STUCK-UP BIG SHOT

A HERO CLUB NOVEL

SIERRA HILL

A COCKY HERO CLUB PRODUCTION

Editor: Missy Boruki
Proofreading by: Piece by Piece Proofreading
Cover Design: Steamy Reads Design

Created with Vellum

INTRODUCTION

Stuck-Up Big Shot is a standalone story inspired by Vi Keeland and Penelope Ward's *Stuck-Up Suit*. It's published as part of the Cocky Hero Club world, a series of original works, written by various authors, and inspired by Keeland and Ward's *New York Times* bestselling series.

DEDICATION

To Vi Keeland and Penelope Ward—you two are incredible. Thank you for this opportunity to be part of your Cocky Hero Club shared world. I loved Stuck-Up Suit so much and am honored to share my story to include Graham and Soraya, and Blackie, too.

1

Sutton

The loud blare of a fire alarm wakes me from a dead sleep.

Jolting upright in an unfamiliar bed, my senses shift to overdrive from the sound of the nonstop alarm, along with the incessant barking of a dog. All I want to do is bury my head under this pillow and howl.

Speaking of howl, why do I hear a dog?

Flipping off my sleep mask, I stare sleepy-eyed and confused around the room, blinking several times to clear the cobwebs and fog as I slowly return from dreamy disorientation to wide awake panic.

"Oh my God! Blackie. Blackie, where are you?"

That's right—there is a dog! And he's not mine. Nor is the comfortable bed or cushy apartment, which is apparently on fire at the moment.

I jump out of the enormous bed, my bare feet landing on the plush carpeting, searching in vain for something to cover myself with. It's early July in New York City, and I'm wearing only a tank and booty shorts I picked up at TJ Maxx at the end of last summer.

Code words: on sale and cheap.

I see a short robe hanging in the guestroom closet. After yanking it from the hook and draping it over my arm, I scan the floor for some slippers. Geesh, I'm very under-prepared for this type of event in the middle of the night.

Finding a pair of slip-ons, I shove my feet in one at a time as Blackie, the sweet old West Highland terrier I'm dog sitting for the next month—who is ironically all white—comes skittering from around the bed, looking up at me with anxious, petrified brown eyes.

"It's okay, Blackie. We'll be fine. But we need to find our way out of here quick."

I bend down to lift the shaking fluff ball as he whimpers helplessly and trembles in my arms. Soothing him with a stroke of my hand over his fur, I jerk upright. As I do, the soft back of my head connects hard against the corner of the dresser, which has spike-like edges, and I yelp in pain. My hand instinctively touches the area, as I rub away the ache that emanates from the spot.

"Ouch! Damn it, that hurts."

Holding the little-bigger-than-a-football sized dog in one arm and the robe draped over the other, I slowly regain my balance and begin maneuvering around in the dark hallway toward the front door. Good grief, can tonight get any worse?

When I accepted this dog-sitting job—a month-long, live-in gig in Graham and Soraya Morgan's Upper West Side home—it seemed like an easy gig. A fire alarm and building evacuation on the second night on duty isn't what I had anticipated in the slightest.

As I fumble with the security alarm and door locks, I realize I'm not sure where the fire exits are on this floor. Since arriving, I haven't had time to explore the building much outside of their apartment. I haven't used an exit other than the artfully-ornate elevator to get to and from this seventh-floor apartment through the main lobby.

Shaking off the concern, I will just follow the other apartment dwellers in search of the exit stairwells. I continue unlatching the locks when a loud knock on the outside of the door scares both me and Blackie. He yips as I let out a startled scream.

"Graham. Soraya. You still in there?" A booming male voice resonates through the wood-paneled door.

I'm not sure who it is, and perhaps under normal circumstances and if I weren't half asleep, I wouldn't open it, but considering the situation, I have no choice but to get out of this apartment. And in doing so, I'll take my chances with the man outside this door.

I quickly punch in the security code to disable the alarm, unlock the final deadbolt, and with my hand poised on the handle, I turn the knob and swing the door open.

The man in the hallway pulls back sharply, taking an uneven step backward when I come into view. His gaze travels over me from head to toe, stopping ever-so-briefly at my breasts, before returning to my face. The bewildered look in his dark midnight blue eyes belies the question of why I'm standing here in front of him and not Graham or Soraya Morgan, who he clearly expected to see.

There is no spark of recognition or inkling of who I am.

I am apparently a complete stranger to him.

But I sure recognize him.

Oh, boy, do I ever.

It's Miles Thatcher.

My childhood friend, Melodie's older brother.

The very same man who kissed me in Melodie's room the day of her funeral seven years ago.

A kiss he seems to have forgotten. And I'm a woman he doesn't even remember.

Even with this weird and unexpected reunion, my heart strums wildly in my chest and out of control at the sight of Miles in the doorway.

Holy smokes.

Did I hit my head harder than I thought? Because why else would Miles have materialized in front of me out of the blue, as if I've just conjured him out of my dreams?

What in the world is he doing here?

Although his appearance doesn't suggest it, maybe he's with the fire department sent to rescue me. Like the way he rescued me from that tree so many years earlier.

"Button, how in the hell did you get that far up there?" Miles's tone is a mixture of amusement, disapproval, and maybe even a little pride, considering the height of which I've climbed the big oak tree on the Crispin's front yard.

I grasp tightly to the limb, afraid to look down, but also not wanting Miles to know I'm a scaredy-cat. He would tease me mercilessly for days, maybe weeks to come. As do boys his age to little girls nearly six years their junior. It's the way of the world. As a skinny, brace-faced, skinned-knee twelve-year-old, I'm just an invisible pest to the hometown hero, Miles Thatcher.

Everyone in town worships him, as do I, which makes this an impossibly embarrassing predicament to be stuck in a tree while Miles and his sister, Mel, look on from ten feet below.

"Are you stuck up there, Button? Need my help?"

His loud bark breaks through my teenage memories, splintering them to pieces like broken glass. "Who the hell are you?"

2

S*utton*

Blackie chooses this moment to bark, and it draws my attention down to the hysterical white fur ball in my arms. Or maybe I'm the one that's hysterical. I mean, I'm standing in front of my teenage crush in my summer pajamas as an alarm sounds in an unfamiliar apartment hallway.

Or perhaps it's just the alarm bells I hear in my own head at the sight of Miles.

I stand in silent awe, confusion etched in my brows and a gaping mouth, about to respond to his question. But he doesn't seem to have time for my idiotic behavior.

"Never mind," Miles grunts impatiently, peering around me to check to see if anyone else is in the apartment. "We need to get out of here. Are Graham and Soraya here with you?"

I stare blankly back at him until he extends an arm and

grabs me, clasping his warm hand around my wrist where the robe loops over, precariously dangling there. I catch it just as it slips, and he tugs me forward, my feet tripping over themselves to keep up. The door swings shut behind us as I follow Miles, his strides long and purposeful, hellbent on getting out of here and to safety.

A few other occupants emerge from their apartments, Miles nodding after them, but remaining quiet and singularly focused. If he notices that his hand is still glued to my arm and I'm having to take three steps for every one of his, he doesn't show it. He just continues down the corridor and around the corner to the stairwell marked *Exit*.

Aha—so that's where it is! A coat of relief settles over the panic that's been pushing through my bloodstream for the last five minutes.

Miles bursts through the heavy door into the stairwell, now crowded with bodies, most dressed in their bedtime attire, as we descend the seven flights of stairs before pushing through to the exterior street-level exit at the back of the building.

We exit into a very crowded alleyway, where people of all age groups congregate and mill about, some chatting or in frantic tears, some on their phones, and others looking just plain exhausted. I get corralled to the left, while Miles heads toward the opposite side of the building.

I lose track of him in the crowd and work my way through the maze of people while still holding Blackie in my arms. After rounding the corner, Blackie and I stand in front of the building and take in the scene. The street is now littered with bystanders and gawkers, fire engines sit parked along at the sidewalk, and the fire crew works to assess the situation.

I shiver out of shock, not chill, and crane my neck to see

if I can spot Miles again, but he seems to have disappeared entirely. I look down at my appearance and then realize how exposed I am and no longer have the robe I brought with me.

"Miss?" A man's voice startles me, as I turn to find a large, strapping fireman at my side. "Why don't you wrap this around you? It'll help regulate your temperature, which is probably low because of the shock you're in."

He hands a blanket to me, which I gratefully accept. In my daze, I try to figure out how I'll cover myself while still holding Blackie, since I didn't grab one of the leashes hanging in the hall closet before rushing out. Then I remember that the dog obeys the basic commands of sit, stay, come, fetch, etc., according to the quick description from Graham before he left on vacation. I take a chance and set Blackie down on the ground for a moment, then I crouch down and say, "Sit, Blackie. Stay."

Pleasantly surprised and relieved that he does what he's told, I tug the blanket around my shoulders. While still crouched down, I look around the sidewalk, peering through a sea of legs to see if I can find the robe I brought with me. It must've slipped off my arm as we moved through the crowd.

Not spotting it anywhere within visual distance, I'm about to pick Blackie back up in my arms, when a red NYFD truck with lights flashing and an earsplitting emergency siren blasting, barrels to a stop on the street next to the sidewalk. The screech of the brakes is loud and spooks my scared little buddy. Blackie slips through my hands and tears off down the sidewalk, through the throng of people milling about.

Just like that, he's gone in a flash, and I can't see him anywhere.

"Blackie!" I yell, pushing to a stand and swiveling to search the area. "Blackie, come back!"

A feeling of panic surges from the depths of my stomach, filling me with more fear than I have ever felt in my entire life.

Oh my God, I've just lost the Morgan's dog.

I am the worst dog sitter in the world.

And I am so going to be fired.

3

Miles

WHAT A CLUSTERFUCK. I'm tired, stressed, and now I'm dealing with this crazy shit in the middle of the night.

I've barely slept yet tonight, and now this?

The minute we get outside, I'm swallowed up within the crowd, and the girl and the dog that were in Graham's apartment are nowhere to be found. Just as well. I don't need to babysit anyone tonight. But I am curious as to who she is. She seems vaguely familiar to me.

Standing in an alleyway in the back of the building, safe for the time being, I type out a message to Graham to find out who the young woman is in his apartment.

Me: Strange night. Who the hell is in your apartment?

I know he said he'd be out of the office for a while, something about a family vacation. But, aside from the additional workload he gave me, I didn't pay it much attention or ask him questions about where he was going. At the time, I was in the middle of a curating a lucrative investment deal and had just given Graham and the board members the pitch, which was unanimously approved, by the way.

It's one of my bigger accomplishments in my fourth year with the firm, and the most lucrative so far this year, and I am pretty damn proud of that.

In fact, Graham, being the head of Morgan Financial Holdings, where I am a senior investment advisor, asked me to fill in for him during his absence. Not only do he and I work together, but we're also good friends, former college classmates from Wharton, and now neighbors. I initially worked for a different firm after graduation and a brief overseas trip out of the country to clear my head, but was soon recruited by Graham, where I've been the past four years. Graham's the real deal, a great guy and a good friend.

That's why I'm doing my due diligence out of loyalty and friendship to find out who the hot chick is that opened their front door. She is most definitely not their usual house and dog sitter. Far from it. The lady that typically manages things in their absence scares the shit out of me. I think she might be a fire-breathing dragon and enjoys cutting the balls off men.

I was more than a bit surprised to find such a sexy creature in their doorway tonight. In the heat of the moment— all right, yes, I took a quick perusal of her appearance and skimpy attire— I didn't care who she was, only that I wanted to get her out of the building in the event it was burning to the ground.

However, the minute we got outside, I lost sight of the pretty young thing as we wound up getting separated in the crowd. And since then, I've been busy helping some of my elderly neighbors and trying to get in touch with Graham.

She seemed to have gone the opposite direction, and I haven't tracked her down yet.

My phone pings with a response from Graham.

G: She's Ben Schilling's cousin. Watching things while we're gone.

And then a moment later...

G: Wait, why? She didn't burn the place down, did she? Or are you looking to get in her pants?

I clear my throat and wince. I may have a reputation, especially with Graham, who has known me for years, for sleeping around. Call it a hobby of mine. Lately, I've been too invested in building my career and portfolio to want anything serious from a woman. I've had a friends-with-benefits situation going on over the past six-months with Margo, a former colleague, but after tonight, I'm not sure it's worth pursuing any further.

As I glance around and then up at the building, I ponder his other question. While I know the FDNY is on the premises investigating the cause of the alarm, I will not aid in his suspicions about his house sitter or make any assumptions she's to blame. But it is a weird coincidence, right?

I type out a quick reply.

Me: Funny you should ask. . . there's been a building evacuation. FDNY is here. I'm fairly certain it wasn't her doing.

G: WTF? A fire? Where is she now? Is my dog okay?

Oh Jesus, I think I've gotten him panicked over nothing.

Me: G, it's fine. There's no smoke or fire that I can tell. And I'm sure she's fine. She carried Blackie down in her arms. Now go back to having fun wherever you are.

Someone bumps into my back, and I'm about to let them have it when I turn to find Mr. Collins, a retired and renowned journalist for the *New York Times*, standing in his bathrobe and house shoes, looking more than a little bewildered. He's confused, searching for his dead wife, who he talks about like she's still living.

I reign in my temper and place a hand on his bony shoulder. "You okay, Mr. Collins?"

The old man glances up at me and nods. "Just a little winded, is all. And I had to leave my bird, Prissy. I hope she's okay. And I can't find my Diana."

I cock my head and give him a sympathetic nod, even though I hate that bird of his and his wife, Diana, has been dead for two years. She squawks like a motherfucker. The bird, not the dead wife. I can hear her two-stories down at breakfast and dinner every day. The bird goes nuts when she isn't fed on time. And honestly, I think Mr. Collins often forgets.

His symptoms are very similar to what I experienced with my Granny, who is now in a nursing facility after putting up a big fight before moving out of our family home in Connecticut.

"I'm sure she'll be fine," I placate, not knowing how tonight will even end up.

The alarm sounded, and we evacuated twenty minutes ago. Meanwhile, firefighters have been running in and out of the building in search of any telltale signs of fire. I crane my neck to look upwards, seeing no immediate signs of smoke or fire. Must be a false alarm.

Which only aids in my frustration and need for sleep. My schedule is packed tomorrow, and I have an important client presentation I need to prepare for in the morning. The time on my phone displays three-thirty a.m. I'd been home and in bed for less than two hours before all this chaos ensued.

Earlier in the night, I'd gone over to Margo's for drinks, our typical weekly event. After our regular fun and dirty fuck, I was preparing to leave her place when she opened a Pandora's Box, starting a fight with me about our relationship status.

When I said, "What relationship status?" she went ballistic. Unbeknownst to me, something changed with her understanding of our arrangement in the past few weeks. And tonight—after I'd fucked her over her kitchen table—she unwisely started lecturing me over my "lack of engagement."

As in, we are definitely no longer on the same page with our fuck-buddies situation. And while I told her early on that I was not serious boyfriend material and I never would be, she seemed to forget that conversation.

So, I got dressed, kissed her cheek, and left her place around one a.m., knowing it would likely be the last time I'd see her again.

On top of that, my week is utter shit. I'm cleaning up a mess one of my junior analysts created with a client that cost us a couple hundred grand. Had I not caught the error, it could've easily been twice as costly of a mistake. I conveniently left that out of my texts to Graham.

And Granny broke her ankle and needed to be restrained, but was otherwise doing well, according to her caretaker.

This isn't the first time Granny has become agitated, and her unwillingness to be helpful causes accidental injuries. It only makes my guilt rise higher, since I'm not there to take care of her and can't get back to my hometown of Mystic, Connecticut as often as I like.

Just like it was seven years ago when I wasn't there for my sister, Mel, when she needed me.

Shit. When will this week end?

Tonight was supposed to help take my mind off things. All I wanted was to get laid and get some sleep. Instead, I stand outside my apartment building with the rest of the tenants, waiting to learn if we'll even be able to return to our own beds tonight.

Blackie's name being shouted and called in a panicked and shrill voice grabs my attention. I swivel my head around, searching in which direction the sound is coming from.

I lean back and peer down the alleyway and see Graham's dog-sitter running up and down the sidewalk, a wool blanket in tow, calling out over and over again for Blackie, frantically stopping to ask each group of bystanders if they've seen him.

Ah, shit.

Her eyes connect with mine, and I can see tears streaming down her cheeks, the panic visible from her expression. A lump lodges in the back of my throat, bubbling up in an angry, unapologetic fireball as I stride toward her.

Instead of helping, I unleash an accusatory attack on this poor girl. My words are full of reproach. I blame my sleeplessness and stress on my reaction.

"How the fuck did you lose Graham's dog? You're supposed to be watching him."

She hiccups and babbles in incomplete sentences, strands of hair flying across her face as her head shakes hysterically. "I didn't grab his leash. . . when the fireman gave me a blanket. . ." *Hiccup. Hiccup.*

"I set him down. . . and then the fire truck. . . oh my God, Miles, please help me find him!"

I'll find it odd later that she called me by name, considering we haven't been properly introduced, but for now, I exhale sharply and nod in resignation.

"*Fuuuuck*," I groan, rubbing my temple with fierce strokes of my fingers before pointing at her. "I'm only doing this for Graham. Not to save your incompetent ass."

She nods in apologetic understanding, and her eyes pierce me with recognition. It reminds me of something from the past. The pleading look. The sadness and sorrow.

Shaking off the strange feeling, I devise a plan. "Which way did he run off? We can head that way together and then split off down the side streets in different directions."

The woman's hand darts out from under the blanket and points to the right. "That way."

"Okay. Let's go find Blackie."

She spins, her slippers slapping against the sidewalk when I snag her wrist to halt her progress. My eyes narrow with censure and brows furrow inward.

"But don't think for one second that I will not mention this to Graham or Soraya. You got that?"

She sniffles, dragging the corner of the blanket underneath her nose. "Yes. I understand."

"Fine. Get yourself together and let's go."

And then she sprints down the street with me trailing behind, feeling like a complete and utter asshole.

But nobody ever said I wasn't.

4

Sutton

WE FIND Blackie safe and sound in the arms of a man named Mr. Collins, who, weirdly enough, is petting him and calling him Prissy.

Miles mutters under his breath how "lucky" and "irresponsible" I am. He even flat out told me he would notify Graham over my incompetence.

None of that matters to me now, because I am overcome with such a profound sense of relief that I can't speak and care little about anything else. Even the heartless words Miles said to me earlier vanish into the background.

Perhaps if I wasn't terrorized over the potential *what ifs* had Blackie not been found, I would argue with Miles as he verbally attacks me for my ineptitude. But instead, my tongue is dry, and I've cried my eyes out over losing, and then subsequently finding, Blackie that I don't utter a word to anyone. Tears blur my vision as I take Blackie into my arms from the old man, and I sob into the dog's soft coat of fur.

It's only a few minutes after our tearful reunion when the FDNY gives us the all-clear signal, having found the culprit of the fire alarm—a faulty wire in the main fuse—and we are given the good news that we can return to our apartments.

I'm exhausted, shaken, and feel like the worst human on the planet.

Although the "all's well that ends well" adage helps stabilize my mood a bit, it is the harsh bite of Miles's assessment of my derelict dog sitting skills that stings like a wasp bite long afterward.

Sadly, I can't even fault him for that.

Under normal circumstances, I believe that something like this wouldn't have happened, because I'm a very attentive individual. I'm a strong and solid student, I remember birthdates of friends and family, and I never forget to mail in payments on time.

I know I wasn't operating as my best self tonight, but I should have been more careful and considered the possibility that Blackie might run off if scared by something. It was my job to take care of him and ensure his safety, and I failed miserably.

~

ODDLY, though, I haven't heard a thing from Graham or Soraya. I assumed the minute we returned to our apartments, Miles would contact Graham and tell him what a horrible job I'm doing in caring for their dog.

I'm surprised I've not received a call asking me to pack

my things and get the hell out of their house. I sat up all night, unable to fall back asleep, nervously waiting on pins and needles for the call that never came. Now, this morning I'm not only tired but stuck in a conundrum of what to do about it. Should I preemptively notify the Morgan's of what happened or leave it be?

I consider my options while baking a quiche in the massive kitchen. My phone sits on the countertop, ready to alert me if a message comes through, as I whisk the eggs into a frothy foam. After I pour the egg concoction and cut-up vegetables into the baking dish, open the oven door, and slide the quiche in, I set the time for sixty minutes and make my decision.

I text Soraya a benign message to test the waters. To see if Miles really did what he said he would do.

Me: Hi Soraya, I hope you are all having a wonderful vacation so far. I just wanted to check in. Besides a little scare last night, which is nothing to worry about. Everything is great. Blackie is doing well.

Technically, it's all the truth, even though a few facts have been omitted. But it gives me peace of mind that I've done the right thing. No harm, no foul, as they say.

I think about Miles and our unexpected reunion and awful interaction last night. Granted, it was under the worst possible circumstances you could imagine, but I was thoroughly confused by his behavior. His attitude was so completely different from the Miles I used to know. The pre-Melodie's death Miles. And the fact that he doesn't remember me feels like a knife to the gut.

After sending the text, I decide to call my friend, Christiana, to ask her opinion about what to do from here and whether I should track down Miles and talk to him or just leave it be.

She answers on the first ring and I begin to tell her everything about the fire-alarm fiasco and running into my new neighbor, Miles.

"Maybe I should have taken that job as the magician's assistant instead," I whine, thinking back on the job offers I'd received before accepting this out-of-the-blue job last week. "At least then, I wouldn't be in this strange predicament."

Before being recommended for this position through my cousin, Ben, I had poured over countless other summer jobs, hoping to find a second job to make ends meet before returning to NYU this fall. But the job had to fit into my current part-time schedule at the small boutique I work at in SoHo. The only one that had some promise was a real honest-to-God magician's assistant, helping an older guy at kid's birthday parties.

Christiana laughs with a lilt of amusement on the other end of the line.

"You? Responsible for flaming swords and knives and shit? Not a chance. You're a bona fide klutz."

"Pffft," I snort, pursing my lips together in a scowl. "I am not. Trip over your own feet *one* time in front of the Biochem classroom, and no one ever lets you forget about it!"

She belly laughs long and hard. "Well, tripping aside, you've proved that you can make animals disappear. Ba-dum-dum."

I wince, crying out in a gasp. "Ouch, that was a low-blow."

"Sorry," she apologizes. "Too soon to joke about Blackie running off?"

I plunk down on a kitchen island chair, twisting my head to find the dog in question sleeping soundly on his bed in the living room. I've been paying him extra attention and showering him with treats today, but I still feel a pang of guilt.

"Yes, too soon. You're just plain cruel," I grumble. "It's bad enough that Miles was so rude and mean last night. I can't believe he's the same guy that kissed me."

I'd told Christiana all about it the minute I called her, sharing the details of the last time I'd seen or spoken to Miles, that he didn't remember who I was when he saw me, and then how demoralizing his words were to me.

He used to be such a nice guy. Now he acts like a stuck-up jerk.

Christiana blows out a breath from the other end of the line.

"Obviously, I can't speak for him or his intentions since I wasn't there. But maybe cut him a little slack. No one ever knows what's going on in someone else's mind."

I snort. "Did you just read that straight from one of our psychology textbooks?"

Christiana and I have been friends for years now, both in the same grad program at NYU. I initially lived with her and her roommate last summer, which helped me save money for the school year and room and board but chose not to this summer for several reasons.

One, I love Christiana with all my heart. She's an incredible friend and brilliant woman, but she is a slob. Plain and simple. I just couldn't deal with the mess she left behind in all our shared spaces. And being that I was the couch-crasher in our living arrangement, I had no right to call her out on it since it wasn't my apartment.

The second reason was her obnoxious roommate, Nadine. She thought she was the Queen Bee and the overlord because her father owned the apartment and therefore dictated how things were to go. I'd asked Christiana at one point how in the world she put up with Nadine's bitchiness, to which she replied, "It's all about the money. I only pay a fraction of the cost, and it beats living at home with my brothers."

Enough said.

Christiana has three brothers, and they are always trying to get involved in her business. They're the worst. Plus, renting in New York City is beyond expensive. That's why this summer, two weeks prior to the end of my spring semester, I'd asked my cousin if I could crash with him until the fall. My scholarships and grad student stipend are enough for tuition and expenses for the school year but doesn't cover the summer months when I'm not in school and need a place to live. And my job at Rags & Tags doesn't bring in enough to pay for rent and other expenses on its own.

Thus, I'd been desperate to find a secondary summer job that worked with my variable schedule and one that affords me the luxury of things like food.

That's how this entire dog-sitting arrangement fell into my lap, if you follow. Ben, who is several years older than me and the son of my mother's cousin, is the one who recommended me to his boss, Graham, when he learned they needed a last-minute pet sitter.

Fate seemed to intervene, in more ways than one. Because here I am, facing this highly unusual reunion with Miles.

"Sutton, don't make it about you, sweetie," Christiana commiserates. "It was just the wrong time, wrong place. Maybe Miles has some serious matters weighing on him, and with the drama of evacuating and whatever else, he lashed out at you. And look, it all turned out fine. No harm, no foul. You have heard nothing from him today, right?"

I heave a sigh. "Not yet. I did just get a response from Soraya saying, 'thanks, having fun.' But I still feel like there's a knife hanging above my head ready to drop the moment Miles says something to Graham. I mean, you didn't see him. He was so angry with me. That's why I want to do something nice for Miles to show him I appreciated his help. But I don't want it to come across as a bribe for him to keep quiet."

"Hmm, I see what you mean. It's a precarious walk along a tight rope. Well, maybe you should make something to bring over to him as a show of gratitude and leave it at that."

"That might work. It's easy, a nice neighborly thing to do, and it doesn't suggest that I'm being pushy or threatening him to keep his mouth shut about what happened."

"Right," she agrees. "If you wanted to threaten, you'd use one of my brothers. They'd get your point across."

The timer on the oven beeps, and I choke out a laugh. "Yes, let's keep your Guido siblings out of this, shall we? Hey, I gotta run. But thank you for your advice. I'll let you know how it goes."

"No problem, sweetie. And who knows? Maybe if the food doesn't work, you can offer something else in exchange. He might enjoy eating something else." She chuckles darkly, and I gasp in mock outrage.

"Keep me posted, babes."

I end the call and remove the quiche from the oven, feeling a little lighter, and less like the ball will drop at any moment. Maybe if I can talk to Miles again, offer him my gratitude, and mention our shared history and get him to remember the kiss we shared, he'll be kinder toward me and less likely to narc on my mistake.

How did this get so complicated?

And how is it I'm so unmemorable to Miles?

After I get showered and dressed, a quick glance at the clock tells me I better hustle it up if I'm going to take Blackie for a quick walk and make it to the store by ten a.m. While I'm not the opener for the day, my boss, Luciana, is a stickler for punctuality.

When I get back from the walk, I eat a piece of my now cooled quiche and wrap the rest up for later. A few minutes of gathering my belongings before I run out the door to get to work, I remind myself I need to plan out how to introduce all of this to Miles.

And figure out whether he'll be happy to find out who I am and how we're connected.

5

M*iles*

I DRAG my exhausted body out of the elevator and blindly make my way down the hallway toward my apartment door, wheeling my suitcase behind me as I go.

Traveling cross-country is never at the top of my favorite things to do list, but in this case, it was well worth the time and fatigue. A new client in San Francisco requested my presence at their quarterly board meeting, at which I outlined just how fantastic their portfolio was doing. I walked away from that meeting a very happy man.

Or at least as happy as I can be when I wake up every day with a sense of dread and deep regret following me around like a dark, ominous cloud.

But the trajectory of positivity I'd amassed from the meeting promptly ended there.

When I arrived at the airport for my return flight to New

York, I learned it was delayed. Which then turned into canceled because of the severe summer weather across the Midwest. Fuck global warming.

My only option was to stay overnight at the airport Hilton. It wasn't so bad at first. I had a place to stay and a decent dinner accompanied by a pint of Guinness, but then I was propositioned by a tranny prostitute named Stella in the lobby bar.

Which, hey, I hold nothing against anyone if you're into that. To each their own. But things got really weird after politely turning Stella down. She kept grabbing for my hand and trying to get me to squeeze her breasts, suggesting how real they felt and all the amazing things she could do with them. And that's when I called it a night.

My flight this morning was on time, and I spent most of the five-hour trip catching up on some work with my inflight WiFi. The minute I touched down at JFK, I cabbed it back to the office to make a staff meeting scheduled at four p.m., which because of Graham's absence, I was in charge of running. I finished the night with a seven o'clock business dinner with Tommy, a client who likes to drink. And when he gets a good buzz on, he likes to sip old, expensive scotch and shoot the shit.

Our meeting ran well over five hours until I finally ordered him an Uber to take him home and cabbed it back home myself. All I want to do now is strip off this suit and tie, slip into some athletic shorts and have one more drink before hitting the hay.

A sticky note with a smiley face on the outside of my door draws me to a stop. With the keys in my grip, poised to unlock the door, I cock my head at the little yellow paper, tearing it off with more force than necessary and giving it a read.

Miles,

Hi! To say thank you for your help retrieving Blackie the other night, I made you a special dinner. Stop by anytime to retrieve it.

Sutton (the Morgan's dog sitter)

I read it curiously, her unusual name niggling at something in the back of my mind. It's different but also familiar somehow. Either way, it's late, and I've already eaten tonight, so I crumple up the note, unlock my door, and then drop it in the wastebasket.

Suspicion trickles down my spine. Have I slept with this woman before? Maybe that's why she seems familiar.

Based on my memory of her the other night, however, and the sexy body of hers in that tiny sleep set she wore, she seems far too young for the likes of me. I would put her around college age, maybe a smidgeon older, but definitely younger by at least five years. It's probably a good guess that we didn't attend college or business school together.

Perhaps she worked for Morgan Financial in the past as a student intern. Graham hires a gaggle of interns every year, providing them great opportunities to learn the investment business. He'd mentioned she's our marketing manager, Ben's cousin, so perhaps there's a chance she'd been in the office, and I've passed her in the hallways.

Who knows? Regardless, I have no time or desire for her antics or niceties. If my suspicions are valid, she's likely trying to butter me up and bribe me so I'll keep my mouth shut and not mention the temporary misplacement of Blackie to Graham.

Honestly, ratting her out was the furthest thing from my mind since the night of the fire alarm, and now that I've had time to reflect, I don't see a point in stirring up trouble. I'll just keep a watch on things and keep an ear to the ground—

or the wall—to make sure she's not getting out of hand. If she throws even one party, I'll be up in her ass so fast. . .

The thought about her ass and being up in it has my dick twitching at the prospect. Shit, I'm not only tired, but I need to get laid soon. I shouldn't be thinking about the hot young dog sitter next door.

Tearing my clothes off and throwing them in the hamper, a whiff of my undershirt suggests I am badly in need of a shower. I take a quick one, ignoring my aching cock, before pulling on my light gray lounge pants, forgoing a shirt, to allow my body to cool down.

After my shower, I pour myself a scotch, neat, and plop down on my sofa with a sigh of contentment. Reaching for the remote next to me, I turn on the television and flip through a few stations until I come to the hockey game highlights.

Nice. I can catch up on the Rangers and then head to bed.

The knock on my door is both alarming and annoying because I have an inkling I know exactly who it is.

Fuck, was she waiting to pounce the moment I returned home?

Christ almighty, all I want is some uninterrupted downtime. Is that too much to ask for?

Swinging my legs off the couch, I rumble with anger as my feet meet the soft wool of the rug, landing harder than necessary. I took no part in decorating my place. When I purchased it two years ago, I hired a high cost and well-known designer who took care of everything for me. She also took care of me —in the bedroom—during the redesign phase. If I recall, she was very competent in all that she did to and for me.

Now turned on once again, I realize the last time I got

laid was the night with Margo, and lack of sex has me even surlier than I typically am on any given night. Let's face it, the woman standing on the other side of this door will catch hell from me tonight because I am not in the mood for company.

Unless she's offering that ass.

Then I might reconsider. I'll have to see how things go.

With a snarl, I unlatch the locks and punch in the security code, swinging the door wide to find just who I expected standing outside the doorway.

"What?" I bark, gaining an evil satisfaction knowing I've startled her as she jumps back a step.

Sutton regains her balance, fumbling with a tower of food containers in her hands, working to ensure they don't topple over. I lower my head, my menacing glare penetrating her soft features, the tight muscle in my jaw twitching as she chews her lips nervously.

Her eyes slowly drift down my bare chest, and then a little lower, before she swiftly lifts her gaze back to meet mine. Her wide-eyed expression is almost comical enough to make me smile because it's obvious she noticed my semi pressed firmly against the thin material of my sleep pants. Good.

For some unknown reason, I enjoy making her feel uncomfortable. She's easy to rile up and agitate. It brings back memories of being a kid and teasing my little sister and her friends, getting them to shriek and laugh and run away as I chased them around the house.

Maybe it'd be fun to chase this hot girl around the bedroom.

My icy glare cuts into her more, and she sways a bit under my scrutiny.

"You realize it's after midnight, don't you? I could've been sleeping."

The covered dishes wobble again in her nervous hands, another Jenga-like jiggle, as she inhales a sexy gasp, her face covered with a sudden blush. Which I dare say, despite the interruption, is rather cute.

She's actually rather cute. No, not just cute. She borders on beautiful.

Pouty, full lips, with an indentation in the bottom center that looks like someone at birth left a thumb in the plushy softness just for fun. A pretty nose that slopes a bit at the tip, making it adorably kissable. Deep hazel eyes that extract more green than gray, with flecks of gold scattered about that seem to express sincerity and honesty. As if they've never held or told a lie.

And her slender neck exposed because her rich auburn hair is piled high in a messy bun, beckons to be skimmed with my fingers and sucked by my lips and tongue.

My body inconveniently reacts even further. My erection grows hard and hot with seething want. Placing my hands in front of my crotch, I do my best to appear bored and irritated with her arrival, as I mentally reprimand myself for taking notice of her physical beauty.

Nope, nope, nope. Not happening, dude.

"Oh. . . hi, Miles. I know it's late. . ." she stammers, her lashes blinking furiously, teeth scraping over her bottom lip again.

My aggravated sigh turns soft, much to my chagrin. "What do you want?"

I hope she'll get to the point quickly if I continue acting like a dick, sending her scurrying away whence she came. I now want more than ever for Sutton just to leave me alone so I can forget the way she seems to bubble hot over my skin, heating me like an icy-hot ointment.

I don't want anyone to get close. It's the way it's been for years and the way it has to remain—the only way I can survive. If being a bastard and a prick is how I accomplish that goal, then so be it.

I am not a man deserving of homemade meals, sweet, apologetic gestures, or kindness. Not after what happened with my Mel.

Not after what I let happen to my baby sister.

Sutton stands in front of me, uncertainty flickering through her eyes as she shifts the dishes to balance in one hand and gives a tiny wave with the other. "Um, so did you get my note?"

I feel a bit of guilt when I roll my eyes and reply with harsh sarcasm, "Yeah, I got it. What are you, like, in high school or something? Needing to pass notes in the hallway?"

Sutton chuckles nervously, perhaps misunderstanding that my mocking criticism is meant to be unkind, not humorous.

"No, of course not. It's just that I couldn't get ahold of you any other way. I made all this food and didn't want it to go to waste."

She shoves the stack of containers toward me, and I stare down at it, unmoving and unwilling to take the bait. My hands clench in fists at my sides before I purposely cross them over my bare chest in defiance.

But this doesn't deter her one bit, and I don't know if that makes me like her more or less or find her more attractive. It's a toss-up at the moment.

Hesitating only for a moment more, she pinches her brows together and frowns disapprovingly before clutching the food to her chest, then skirts past me through my open doorway. Right into my apartment.

I gawk at her audacity but say nothing. I turn to watch her over my shoulder as she makes her way into the kitchen. Finding space on the counter, she sets the containers down before opening the fridge and rummaging around for God knows what.

"Please come in and make yourself at home," I deadpan. "But I'll have you know your efforts are for nothing and the food will just go to waste. I already ate dinner tonight, and I rarely eat meals at home."

She bends over at the waist, the position lifting the bottom of her shorts, so a peek of curvy ass winks at me, as if to say, "*you know you want it*." It begs the question of whether it's the food or the woman I might crave later.

She arranges the containers in the fridge, tilting her head toward me to the side, a smile edging at the corner of her mouth, pity lacing over her pretty lips.

"Well, that's just sad, Miles. Everyone should have home-cooked meals every once in a while. My family used to have Sunday dinners, and we'd eat leftovers for days."

Out of nowhere, a pang of grief hits me squarely in my chest. The memory of my baby sister standing on a stepstool at the stove, Granny next to her in her apron as she instructed Mel on the finer points of making her famous fried chicken. To this day, I don't think I've ever found a replacement for Granny's food.

"Miles, are you okay?"

I blink, startled that Sutton is now so close, the warmth of the memory immediately fading and turning cold. My gaze drops to where Sutton places a gentle hand on my forearm, where the soft brush of her fingertips sends darts shooting up my arm and into my chest.

This does not help matters one bit. I don't need her kindness, and I don't want her pity.

Wrenching my arm away from her, I once again cross my arms at my chest. Her smile dims. No longer is there empathy or sympathy in her bright eyes, now they're flooded with sadness.

Fuck me, I'm such an asshole.

Clearing my throat, I shake my thoughts free. Goddamn, this woman. She's making me out to be the bad guy here. I never even invited her in. She's an uninvited interloper, forcing me to feel things I don't want to feel.

But the warmth still lingers where her fingers wrapped around my arm. Human touch—at least the type that doesn't lead to sex—is something I haven't had for months. Maybe even years.

Ever since Mel died.

"Yeah, yeah. . . I'm fine, just tired, Sutton, and I want to go to bed. I was on a business trip and have had a busy day. I just really need you to go home."

Disappointment clouds her pupils, and her cheeks flush pink. Her hand flits in the space between us.

"Oh, oh, of course. I'm sorry. I didn't mean to impose. I just really wanted to express my gratitude for your help the other night finding Blackie. And I swear, I'm not usually that irresponsible. It's not an excuse, but with the chaos and circumstances—"

I interrupt her, circling back toward the door, hoping she'll get the hint and follow. "Whatever. No need for explanations. It's over and done with."

I hold the door open for her and turn to find her still rooted in the same spot, and I groan, dropping my chin to my chest. She's stalling and obviously wants to say something else but hesitates.

"Miles, I um, I also wanted to talk to you about—"

I know what she's about to say, so I interrupt her again. "Sutton, it's cool. I didn't and won't mention anything to Graham about Blackie running off. And unless something else happens, I don't plan on getting you fired."

She blanches, either not expecting me to say that or surprised I would protect her in that way. Whatever the case, I wave my hand and work to usher her out the door.

Taking a few steps forward, she pauses, biting down on that full lower lip again, which I can't stop staring at, then she finally makes her way to the doorway. As she passes, I catch a whiff of her light, sweet scent. A lemony-fresh soap smell and something sweet. Like a sugar cookie.

Another memory jostles loose in my head, taking me back to the day of Mel's funeral. I was standing over her casket, my eyes red-rimmed, and my body filled with rage and anger. Someone came up behind me, as my head fell between my shoulders, and I felt the gentle pressure of a hand on my back. It was warm and provided a sense of peace. And somehow her scent evokes that same feeling.

Odd. I fucking need some sleep.

"Thank you, Miles. I appreciate that. I really need this job. And thanks again for your help." She takes a step and stops, turning to look over her shoulder at me. "I left reheating instructions on the lids and my number in case you have questions. Feel free to leave the empties outside my door whenever you're done. Good night, Miles. I hope I'll see you around."

I close and lock the door behind her. Leaning against the doorframe, my body and mind weary from the exchange.

There's something so familiar about Sutton, but I just can't place it. Somehow her presence has evoked strange memories from the past.

The memories of my sister keep popping up more frequently for some reason. And then it dawns on me. I rush over to the wall calendar, flipping over the page from last month that is still displayed and see the July date.

Sure enough. It's not Sutton that's manifesting all these recollections. It's because next week is Mel's birthday.

The date hits me like a semi-truck, plowing through my head, crashing into the pit of my stomach.

July sixteenth.

Next week would have been my baby sister's twenty-fifth birthday.

But, just as I've done for the past seven years, I'll be celebrating her alone.

The sister I left and walked away from.

Another family member I couldn't save.

6

S*utton*

Throughout the next few days, I've only run into Miles three times during various encounters around the building. Each one has been awkward, at best, and humiliating from my perspective.

And at no point in those impromptu run-ins have I been able to tell him about our history and my friendship with Melodie. And it feels like I'm lying to him because of it.

Speaking of awkward, I see Miles again this morning when Blackie and I are out in front of the apartment building.

While I'm not a morning person, I've become accustomed to getting up early to take Blackie outside for his morning constitution. I never realized what a hassle it is to be a city dweller and own a dog.

Where I grew up, we had yards for dogs to run around

and areas they could go to do their business. Not city sidewalks where the moment you bend down to clean up doggie doodie, you get bumped in the ass by a passerby and inevitably find your hand covered in poo.

Trust me, it happens.

"Come on, Blackie. Please just poop already," I prod, as Blackie takes his own sweet time sniffing every tree stump and piece of land covering the entire block. "It's not like this is unfamiliar territory for you, bud. Been there, done that. Now, can you get on with it? I have to go to work."

We generally stroll up and down the block first thing in the morning before breakfast. Then I take Blackie out again before heading off to my job at Rags & Tags. In the evenings after his dinner, we take a long walk down to the park, just a few blocks away. This neighborhood is conveniently located in the Upper West Side with Central Park practically right down the street.

The area also boasts some pretty nice restaurants—including a fancy Italian place which is way out of my price range—and a few fun and not so fancy pubs and cafes.

Just the other night, I shamelessly flirted with the bartender, Russ, at the Horse and Carriage. After one-too-many margaritas and strong encouragement (a.k.a. pressure) from Christiana and our other friend, Taylor, I struck up a conversation with Russ, and one thing led to another, and I gave him my number.

Although my dating experience isn't all that impressive or vast—mainly because I'm overly cautious and extremely picky—when I do feel an attraction, I'm not shy about seeing where it goes.

I don't date much these days. Not that I'm not interested in meeting someone, or someday finding my soulmate, but dating takes a lot of time. During the school year, I'm focused on studying and working, and I don't have extra time for anything more than infrequent hookups.

Realizing how much time we've spent already, I try to hurry my furry-little buddy along. "Are you going to take all day? Some of us have jobs to get to."

Blackie blinks up at me as if to say, "*Slow your roll, sista. You can't rush excellence.*"

I snicker at this and adjust the leash in my hand, extracting my phone from my back pocket to read the news while the dog does his own communicating with his world of scents and smells.

There are texts from both Ben and Christiana that came in last night after I'd crashed for the night, falling asleep in bed while watching a Netflix episode of *The Great British Baking Show*.

I read Ben's first.

Ben: Hey, cuz. Doing anything next Saturday? My company has a volunteer event, and we're drumming up help. It's for a teen homeless shelter. LMK.

I smile down at my phone like a loon. Ben is such a sweetheart. While I was crashing on his couch and searching for jobs, I'd mentioned how I really wanted to find something to help wayward teens because of the special place it holds in my heart. Mainly due to what happened with Melodie.

There isn't a day that goes by when I don't think about or miss my friend. We were best friends throughout elementary, middle school, and the first part of high school. When I look back, there's not one single event during those years where Mel and I weren't together. The thought has my heart squeezing in anguish. It also makes me curious why Miles doesn't seem to recognize me as the girl who used to be his shadow. I realize I've changed a lot since the last time we spent any time together, but I practically lived at his house during my formative years.

Mel and I met when we were five years old and enrolled in tadpole swim lessons through the YMCA. We both loved the water, and as we grew older, we both swam on swim teams, making the varsity team as freshmen in high school.

During those summers, when we were gangly, pimple-faced teenagers, we'd head to the J. Burkley Public Pool outside of town where her brother was a lifeguard.

It's there that we both experienced our first crushes. Those summers were the best.

What Mel didn't know, and something I'd kept a secret from her all that time, was that my first crush came well before the summer of our freshman year.

My first crush blossomed when I was in sixth grade, when my twelve-year-old self fell head over heels, madly in love with the handsome seventeen-year-old Miles Thatcher.

I remember leaving our Barbie dolls in a box never to be played with again, replacing them with hitting up the local mall and hanging out in Mel's basement. We'd listen to music, watch movies, and spend time with Miles and his friends. Well, that's a stretch. What we did was watch Miles and his entourage play video games all day long. Mel and I were always in the background, like wallpaper, garnering no attention from them whatsoever.

From my perch on a recliner, I'd watch his biceps flex as he easily and deftly maneuvered the controller in his hands. He'd been taller than his friends, more built and muscular —which made him every girl's dream date.

I became enthralled with the shape of his arms and shoulders, which were well-defined from spending his summer playing baseball and lifeguarding. Mel and I would go with their grandmother to watch him play during the summer league games.

He was by far the hottest older boy in our town.

And the only one I ever dreamed about kissing.

But by the time I got to high school, Miles was already in his sophomore year at Yale, leaving Melodie behind at home with their grandmother, and me with a crushed and broken heart.

That's about the time when our friendship changed. Mel grew more distant little by little until one day, our friendship was just gone. Looking back, perhaps it was Miles leaving home that was the catalyst for Mel's downward spiral. Whatever the cause, I still feel remorse over not being there for Mel when she needed me.

That's why I'm in school to become a social worker, and why this volunteer event would mean so much to me.

Glancing up from my phone's screen, I see some action starting to happen as Blackie squats next to a tree he's been loitering around for the last five minutes, and I smile with relief.

"Finally," I groan.

But that relief is short-lived, and everything happens in a slow-motion reel, like that paper towel commercial where the guy is carrying a fresh-baked lasagna casserole in his hands and he trips, sending the food flying across the kitchen floor.

Which is exactly what happens to me.

From my peripheral vision, I see Miles striding out of the front door of the building, his messenger bag wrapped securely around his broad torso, his hands occupied with a cup of coffee and his phone. His head is down, so he doesn't notice Blackie or me, but I can't let this chance pass me by. I want to grab his attention. Because it's important that I change his opinion of me. For some reason, he seems to find me annoying.

"Hey, Miles! Good morning," I say and wave enthusiastically, but my greeting falls on deaf ears because he doesn't hear or see me. In his ears, he's wearing earbuds.

Well, that just won't do.

I take a step forward, hoping to get in front of him just enough to flag him down when I realize I haven't sidestepped far enough from where Blackie just dropped his doodie. My flip-flop slides right into the steaming pile of shit and sticks there.

"Oh shit!" I yelp loudly, trying to extract my foot off the ground, only to find the flip-flop is stuck in the poo and my foot slips out, which is when I lose my balance.

And because I'm now hopping on one foot trying to regain my balance, the other one dangling in the air, Blackie gets excited at my little dance and swings around in front of me, which is precisely when he sees another dog coming toward us.

Blackie surges forward, giving the leash just enough momentum so I'm flying forward, my feet having no traction against the slippery surface, as I land with a thud in a mess of doggie doodoo. The sound is just like you'd imagine, and it squishes hotly between my toes.

If my greeting a moment earlier hadn't garnered his attention, this little uncoordinated act—flawlessly executed, I might add—does the trick to perfection.

Miles stops in his tracks, lifts his head from his phone, and sees me sprawled out, tangled up in a dog leash, brown poo smeared all over my feet and legs, helplessly staring up at him.

Heaven, take me now. I could just die.

"Sutton?" Miles clears his head with a shake as if he can't believe what he's seeing.

And why would he expect to see his neighbor's dog sitter lying on the ground covered in shit? Not exactly an everyday occurrence.

"What the hell are you doing down there?"

There's nothing I can say or do at this point to make me appear sane or rational, so I simply lift a hand in the air and shrug with a smile.

I just as quickly drop said hand when I see it's been painted with dog feces. Oh, gross.

Wiping away the shit the best I can on the ground, I snare the flip-flop from the goop with my fingers, as Blackie sniffs at my hand with an upturned nose, as if to say, "*lady, you stink.*"

Miles opens his leather bag and pulls out a bottle of hand sanitizer and a tissue, gingerly handing them to me, which I gladly accept.

"Christ almighty, Sutton, you're fucking a mess."

I'm not sure if he means that literally or figuratively—or maybe both?

Miles gives me another judgmental perusal, his eyes roaming over my body, and for a moment I think he's about to say something else. But, instead, he shakes his head brusquely, turns abruptly, and walks down the street toward the subway entrance.

And I'm left covered in shit and feel like it too.

So much for changing his opinion of me.

7

S*utton*

After the great doggie doodoo debacle, I don't see Miles again until Thursday night when I'm in a much cleaner state of appearance. In fact, I'm freshly showered and wearing a one-piece bathing suit on my way down to the building's indoor pool and fitness center.

Before leaving on their vacation, Soraya gave me a tour of their building and showed me all the amenities I could use if I were so inclined. The apartment complex boasts a large fitness center, including a workout room, a sauna, and a full-length indoor swimming pool and spa.

Could it get any better than that?

Why, yes, it can.

Because as I walk out the door of the women's shower and dressing room, I pass by the workout room, where I not only see Miles, but I'm treated to the view of a very sweaty and very shirtless Miles lifting weights.

It's official. Thursday night is now my favorite night of the week.

Good God, the man is ripped and chiseled sight to behold.

Miles is fit in a way that only the most disciplined men who work out daily can get. His body is lean and tapered, with impressively broad shoulders, flat washboard abs, and has that perfect V-cut, which dips indecently into his gym shorts. My tongue tingles at the thought of running down the smooth lines of that *V*.

And unlike the other night when I stood in front of a shirtless Miles, this time I gawk unnoticed, without interruption, at his svelte body. Miles is so busy with his set, his side profile facing the mirror in front of him and not toward me, he doesn't notice where I stand hidden behind the gym door.

It's the one and only time I've ever wanted to go unnoticed by Miles.

I take the time to peruse the length of his solid body, enjoying the way his muscles chord and bunch tight with every rep he does. The sweat pours from him, dripping down his chest, neck, and back. Clearly an indication of how long and hard he's been working out.

Once he's done with the bicep curls, he reracks the weights, reaches for a towel hanging over the barbell and wipes the perspiration from his face with a masculine groan. And like a heat-seeking missile, the sound of that groan finds a target between my legs.

My mind goes wild, as I clench my thighs together, grabbing the doorframe for support to keep myself from falling, or worse, touching myself.

My gaze lowers to the fit of his nylon gym shorts hanging loosely at his hips, and my eyes roam over the curves and slope of his perfectly sculpted ass. Holy hell, I've never ogled a man like this in my life. I'm not shy when it comes to my sexuality or the men I'm with, but this is different. I've never just stared and enjoyed the view.

Miles, still unaware of my creepy presence, bends forward at his waist and picks up a different set of larger weights. My mouth dries up like a desert at the view. His calves flex, the veins popping at the intensity of his movement, his thighs bulking as he lifts the new set of weights.

There is no other way to describe what is happening to me physiologically than to say I'm getting hot and bothered. I continue to watch his slow, intentional moves as he straddles the incline bench now, my eyes locking onto the visible bulge outline in his shorts.

A little squeak of excitement escapes past my lips, and it's loud enough to gain attention. Miles lifts his head from the bench, his eyes flare in surprise when he discovers me hiding around the corner.

Oh, crap. I've been caught.

Slapping a hand over my betraying mouth, I flail to the side and out of sight around the corner. Flattening my back against the wall as if I'm a secret agent on a mission. My heart pounds wildly and tries to break free from my chest.

Thump thump thump.

I waste no time and run down the short corridor to the door leading into the pool and fling it open. Rushing to the far corner, sucking in a lungful of chlorine-scented air as I go, I flop down at the edge of a lounge chair and smack my hand against my forehead.

"Way to go, Sutton. You idiot," I scold myself in a censorious tone.

Taking a few moments to catch my breath, I remove the towel I'd wrapped around myself and head to the pool's edge. Since I'm on the far end, there's no easing into the water, so I plug my nose and jump into the deep end.

Feels reminiscent of how I do most things in life. I just jump in, feet first.

The warmth of the water covers me, and the beautiful underwater silence blacks out all the surfaced noise in my head. Noise about Miles. Thoughts about what to do once the Morgan's return home, and I need to find new living arrangements once more.

At least by their return date, I'll have money saved up for the fall when school starts again.

School has me thinking about Christiana, who called me earlier today to ask me if I want to go out with her tonight to celebrate one of our mutual friend's birthday. Not taking no for an answer, she reminded me I need to go out and live it up now before I'm buried in books, lectures, and writing papers in September. Guess I'm going out tonight.

The empty pool is luxurious. I haven't been for a swim in months. I think about what it must cost to live in a place like this as I take smooth strides across the length of the pool, the water rippling around me as I stroke and paddle, easing into my old routine. Miles sure has come a long way from our humble beginnings in Mystic to afford a place like this.

Mel would be so proud of him and what he's accomplished.

I continue swimming, enjoying the quiet and serene sense of being submerged in the water. The gentle lick of cool water over my limbs as I glide through the chlorine-blue pool lulls me into a peaceful trance, as I swim from one end to the other.

With my face underneath the water's surface, my hands reach out to touch the rounded cement curve of the pool's edge. I flip around, pushing off with my feet and back toward the other end. I've counted fifteen laps so far, and I'm hoping to get in ten more before I jump in the sauna and then shower and get ready to go out tonight.

Something catches my attention above the pool's surface as I turn my face to the side, breathing in and breathing out. Without goggles on, the water stings my eyes when I open them, and I can't see very clearly. I lift my head from the water and wipe off my eyes, and my breath stalls when I see a pair of men's feet at the pool deck.

Miles sits down at the edge and dangles his feet and a good portion of his legs over the side, as I swim up to greet him.

He's blurry as I stare at him through wet lashes, but oh good heavens, even in a blurry state, the man is so dang hot. He must've showered off before coming in because he smells soapy-clean, his hair wet and slicked back and out of his face. It only highlights his tanned features and square jawline that has a sexy, scruff covering his rugged jaw.

His voice is low, deep, and so very masculine. "Hello, Sutton. You're looking cleaner than the last time I saw you."

A hint of amusement dances in his eyes and a barely-there stretch of a smile plays at his lips. By comparison, my face breaks into a huge stupid grin, and I giggle with a big shrug.

"Hey, Miles. Not being covered in dog shit is quite an improvement, for sure." I splash him so the water laps at his shin. "How was your workout?"

He flicks his toes up and gives me a return splash, and I don't miss the way his lips edge up into a smirk. The mischief bouncing in his blue eyes tells me he saw me watching during his workout. I wonder how long he knew I'd been watching.

Miles lowers himself into the pool, easing slowly into the water. I watch his torso dip under the waterline, his biceps bulging as he lets go of the side.

My tongue darts out to sweep over my bottom lip, wicking away the trace of wetness there, and I notice his gaze zoom to my mouth before flicking back to my eyes.

"You tell me, since I think you saw most of it?"

I wear a look of confusion, glancing around the space as if it's the first time I've ever seen it. "Huh?"

Miles dunks his head underwater and then pops back up, his hand swiping his hair out of his face before his smile unfurls before me, his brows lifted knowingly.

And for all that's holy, that smile is the same one he employed with all the girls back in the day. The one that exudes charm, arrogance, and straight-up sex appeal. It sends a current of electricity coursing through my body, which is a really bad thing when you're near water. I feel like I could easily get electrocuted and drop dead of shock from too much of this Miles.

The flirty, sexy Miles.

I laugh nervously and chew my lip.

"Do you swim as your regular workout?"

I feel the color bloom over my skin, the flush budding and mapping every visible part of me out of embarrassment and the sensual heat that passes between us.

Deciding I need to move to gain some distance from him for fear I'll make an even greater fool of myself, I push off the bottom of the pool and swim on my back, leisurely stroking my arms overhead as I float over the rippling of the water. "I've come down a few times. It's more nostalgic than a workout. It reminds me of my high school swim team. But that was a long time ago."

Miles gives me a dubious look. "Right. . . so long ago."

I want to slap the water hard at my stupidity over bringing up the swim team. The one sport I did with his sister. The sister Miles doesn't remember that I know or was friends with. I should tell him. Come clean about how I know him and Melodie.

But I play it off, laughing shortly at his comment about my age and continue with my strokes and flutter flicks, slowly moving further and further away from him. Along with the chance to tell him about our past.

And then he pushes off, his long, lean body easily catching up to me as he swims alongside me. My belly does its own version of flutter kicks as we glide across the length of the pool, completely in sync with one another, our strokes in even patterns of movement.

When we reach the other side, our bodies mere inches apart, we turn to face each other. I blink the water out of my eyes, lifting my gaze to drink in his beautiful blue eyes, which now narrow down at me.

His tone is abrupt, almost accusatory, and his statement is a delayed reaction of sorts. "My sister used to be a swimmer too."

I gulp, holding onto my breath wondering if he's finally put it together and realizes who I am. And if not, now would be as good of a time as any to tell him.

Miles squints at me with wordless assessment, cocking his head side-to-side, as if trying to figure me out.

And then he goes and says it. And I want to drop my head in shame.

"You seem so familiar to me. Have we ever. . .?"

"No," I raise my gaze back to his face again, ardently shaking my head. "Never."

Technically, that's the truth. We haven't done what I think he's referring to. No matter how many times in my teenage dreams we had, we've never been intimate or had sex. And I choose not to count the kiss we shared the day of Mel's funeral.

At least, not in the way he's suggesting.

Lord knows, if we had sex back then, I would be pretty pissed off right now if he didn't remember me. It's bad enough that my face doesn't even ignite a spark of recognition with him. But if we had gotten down and dirty, and he'd seen me naked, and not remember me? Ouch, that would sting.

Miles nods, his narrowed eyes still scan my face for some trace of recognition. I'm obviously not very memorable, which honestly hurts more than I care to admit. But maybe it's a saving grace, keeping me from the hot humiliation that boils over in my belly.

Although he can't figure me out and continues to stare, I have to admit, it feels fantastic to have his attention on me. And I should tell him. Right now. Right this very instant, I should open my mouth and tell him about my friendship with Mel, and our shared past together. Say to him that he's not crazy and that I seem familiar because I am familiar to him. That we kissed before—the most perfect kiss in the world—even if it happened on one of the worst days of our lives.

But someone must have poured glue over my tongue. Because as I search for the words to tell him, they clump together and get stuck in my throat.

And then, without preamble, he shrugs and says, "Come on. I'll race you."

I'm thoroughly confused by this change of events as he looks back to me over his shoulder, giving me a wink and with an expression that says, "*You scared*?" and I glare at him.

"You're on."

We both set our feet to the wall, hanging on with tight grips of our fingers, ready to push off at the go.

"On your mark. . ." he says, and it shoots a thrill down my spine. I haven't raced for years, and it brings back so many cherished memories.

Memories of all the good times with Mel and me on the swim team. The two of us at competitions, of summers at the public pool, and of the man that now waits to show off his competitive side. A man who was once just a nineteen-year-old lifeguard that I crushed on for years.

"Get set. . . go!"

Let's face it. There really is no competition in this race because Miles is a foot taller than me, has arms that sweep long and overhead, giving him a distinct advantage as he eats up the distance, leaving me in his wake. But none of that matters in the grand scheme of things, because even though I swim and kick as fast as I can, I won't be able to make up the distance between us.

The most I can do is just watch, panting after him over the way his lean arms, and powerful legs carry him along, until he reaches his destination in record time.

The guilt floats along with me over my lie of omission. It's heavy, and the weight tugs on me like an anchor, weighing me down with a drowning sensation. I've never lied to anyone before, not even my parents. It tastes bitter, and I want to cough it out like chlorine water before it chokes me. And I realize if I don't do something soon to dislodge it, to expel that lie, it will most certainly drown me.

When I finally make it to the end, I find Miles already

hanging against the pool's edge, his elbows hooked behind him to partially exposing his torso, and he wears an arrogant grin. It's smug and victoriously gloating.

Before I can stop myself, I dip my palm into the water and retract my arm, arcing it forward to splash him.

He laughs with a sputtering noise, swiping his palm over his face to dispel the water.

"You are such a stuck-up big shot, aren't you?" I snark.

He pushes himself up over the edge and grabs his towel from the chair, running it over his wet hair before wrapping it around his waist. Miles tips his head toward me before heading into the locker room door.

"I never said I was anything else," he replies, shrugging a shoulder in my direction. "And you might want to get some practice in for next time I see you. Later, Sutton."

I'm about to say something before he leaves, desperate to keep this exchange going. Wanting to open up and talk about swimming, and Mel and life before she died.

But it's pointless. It would serve little purpose but to expose me as a liar, humiliate me, and drudge up the past Miles is obviously trying hard to forget. Memories and a past from a small seaside town that only holds harsh memories and bitter ends.

The finality of friendships, family, and a young life gone too soon.

I'm not dumb enough to unearth old wounds when I'm trying to forge something new with Miles.

Because maybe this is fate reuniting us. And whether or not Miles knows it, perhaps there's something positive to be gained out of this reunion.

8

Miles

GRAHAM CALLS me on Friday morning to see how things are going, particularly with the new client from San Francisco that I just bagged last week. I'm barely off the subway and heading into the office building when I take the call.

"Good morning, G-man," I answer, smiling to the woman walking next to me and gesturing for her to go in front me as I hold the door open. She smiles, checking me out with an appreciative glance, as I return the favor. My eyes remain glued to the sway in her hips down the corridor toward the elevators.

When a woman smiles at me seductively, nine times out of ten, I will use that to my advantage and act. Like get her number and text her later to hookup. But I'm not feeling my typical flirtatious self today after yesterday's weird encounter with Sutton in the pool.

Hooking up with anyone else holds no appeal to me this morning as I head up to my office, Graham talking in my ear about trades and profitability, but my mind only on the woman staying in his apartment.

"Hey, I received those documents you sent over about the new client. I reviewed, signed, and returned them to you last night. They should be in your inbox this morning. Impressive job, Miles. Another big account that will help grow our portfolio. I'm proud of you, man."

It's rare you hear praise from the top dog in this cutthroat business, but Graham is a fucking outstanding leader. He built this business from the ground up and continues to make it flourish. I believe that is because of the talent he possesses, along with the people he hires. He also doles out praise on the regular, but this particular compliment has me strutting like a peacock because I've worked my ass off to bring in the business. It also feels nice being recognized not only as a top producer in his business but also as his friend.

"Thanks, G. I appreciate that. I'm just heading into my office now and will have Monica print out the docs and have them filed. How's your vacation? Are you getting much relaxation time?"

There's a soft huff across the line. "I wish. We're on the go every fucking day. Soraya and Chloe are constantly wanting to be everywhere at once, checking out every historical site, cathedral, and museum ever built. Thank God we left Paris behind us. We just arrived in the south of France where we'll be for the next five days. Tomorrow, we're heading out on a sailboat, and we'll just relax onboard and enjoy the ocean and sun's rays."

I sigh wistfully. "Fuck, man, don't rub it in. That sounds spectacular, and if anyone deserves it, you do."

"Thanks, bro. You know the only reason I'm able to take this much time off is that I'm confident you're keeping things running smoothly. And you're the only one I'm checking in with, not because you need it, but so I have another dude to talk to."

I laugh into the phone, my assistant's head snapping up to give me an arch of her eyebrow as I head into my office. "One too many females ruling the roost for you?"

This garners a groan out of Graham, who is vacationing with both his partner and his daughter. Knowing what I do of Soraya, she doesn't let Graham get away with shit. I think that's why they're such a great match. In fact, I witnessed the two getting into quite the explosive argument one day in the office before they even began dating. And holy cow, anyone who saw those two go at it knew there would be fireworks in their relationship.

"You have no idea, man. Thankfully, Chloe is still young and compliant, and Soraya is writing her *Ask Ida* column remotely. She writes a few hours a day, which gives Chloe and me time to hang out together. It works out pretty nicely. Anyway, I should probably get going unless there's anything else to discuss?"

I hear the underlying plea in Graham's voice. He needs something to keep him busy and occupy his mind. Typical Graham. He's been that way from day one.

Hedging just a moment, I ask the question that's been on my mind since first encountering Sutton the night of the fire. She just seems so damn familiar, yet I can't place her or figure it out, and it's driving me fucking crazy.

"Well, I wanted to ask you one thing about Sutton."

"Our dogsitter?" he asks dubiously. "Okay, what about her?"

"It's nothing bad, man. Calm down."

Placing my bag on my desk, opening the flap, and extracting my laptop one-handed, I try to decide how best to bring this up without raising suspicions. Graham will give me holy hell if he gets even an inkling I'm interested in Sutton.

Am I? I shake off the thought. While I'm slowly starting to warm up to Sutton and her sweet klutziness, something happens when I'm around her that has me recalling the strangest memories. I don't know what it is. Maybe it's her youth. I'd say she's roughly the age Mel would be. And Sutton has a youthful quality—innocent in a way and cute as a button.

Something clicks in my head. Sutton. *Button.*

Nah, no way is she the same little girl I'd given the nickname to a long time ago. If she were, she would've said something by now.

Graham's voice splinters through the odd thought.

"Is everything okay at home and with Blackie?"

"Yeah, man. Everything is fine. It's just that your dog sitter seems very familiar to me, and I've been trying to place her. Has she worked in the office for you in the past, maybe as an intern or something?"

There's a pause and then a hiss. "Ah, fuck. You didn't sleep with her, did you?"

I've just taken a sip of coffee that Monica, my assistant, left for me on the edge of the desk and nearly spit it out.

"What? No. She's far too young for me. Why would you even say that?"

Graham gives a mocking snort. "I know you, Miles. Young or not, Sutton is a pretty girl, and you have had an assortment of young women since I've known you. I'm sure you've been more than neighborly and made her feel very welcomed."

He's definitely got it wrong there. I've done just the opposite with Sutton, for some inexplicable reason. I don't know what it is about her, but it's like she can see inside my blackened heart and knows who I am.

"Bro, you have it wrong. I was just curious if I've met her before."

"Don't know what to tell you. I'd never met her before Ben introduced us and we interviewed her for the job. You could always go ask him."

I absently scrub a hand through my hair, still a bit damp from my shower this morning, and consider his advice. It shouldn't matter at this point, and I should just let it go, but maybe a conversation with Ben would do me good. I have a few business-related matters I need to talk with Ben about, anyhow.

"Yeah, sure. Maybe I'll do that. I'll let you go, G-man. Enjoy the south of France, you prick. And don't worry about a thing here. Just relax and have fun."

Graham snickers and says goodbye, hanging up, leaving me with the thoughts of Sutton still swirling in my head. I'm a busy man with a shit ton of work to be done. My schedule is packed tight over the next few weeks while Graham is still out of town, and I don't have time to go traipsing around inquiring about the sexy petsitter next door.

Determined to put it out of my mind, I check my calendar and see that I have a meeting scheduled in ten minutes. I open my inbox to follow up on the email Graham sent and decide to forget about Sutton. For now, at least.

There are other priorities in my life that I need to handle, including Melodie's upcoming birthday this weekend and managing things with Granny.

9

Sutton

SATURDAYS ARE busy at the boutique. I've been working part time for Luciana, Lucy for short, the past two years, and although I'm not the only store employee, I think she's come to rely on me as one of her best staff members.

I'm the most reliable, at the very least. Which is why I open the store every Saturday and manage the inventory for her once a month on a Sunday evening. Which is scheduled for this weekend.

"Did you find something that worked for you?" I prod the customer who has been in the dressing room for over fifteen minutes trying on several outfits I put together for her.

I hear a rustling of clothing coming from the small dressing room and spy a stash of garments hanging over the top, as I wait patiently for her to finalize her decision.

While I wouldn't consider myself a fashionista in any sense of the word, I enjoy helping others find clothing that flatters and makes them feel good about themselves.

After a few more minutes, the woman opens the door, arms loaded with a pile of clothes and hair in disarray. But she looks more happy than disgusted, which is always a good sign that I did my job well.

"You were so right. This purple blouse fits so nicely, and the color does look good on me." The woman beams with gratitude as she hands me the items to ring up.

I smile back at her. "I'm so glad you liked it. The color is a bit loud on the hanger, but I knew it would look great with your complexion."

Walking over to the front register, I place the items on the counter. "Is there anything else you need today? We have a great selection of accessories and shoes if you want to complete the outfits."

I tap my chin with my index finger and lift my eyebrow with an idea. "In fact, we just got in some new hoop earrings that would look fantastic with that dress."

Rounding the corner, I spin the rotating display and find the pair of earrings I have in mind, and then hand them to her while pointing to the mirror above the display. She cocks her head in consideration for a moment before she holds them to her ear in front of the mirror to see what they look like. She smiles and nods.

"You're so good at this. You should get a raise," she remarks candidly, which has me chuckling as I take the earrings and ring up her purchases.

Since Lucy is across the shop, rearranging some displays, I make sure my voice is loud enough for her to hear.

"Did you hear that, Lucy? I should earn more money."

A dainty laugh comes from the back as the customer looks at me inquisitively.

Nodding toward Lucy, who has a price gun in her hand, I say, "That's my boss. She owns the shop."

Lucy gives an appraising glance over the woman's purchases and grins. "Don't give her any more credit than what's required. I taught her everything she knows."

We all laugh, the way insiders laugh at a joke, and I finish ringing up the clothing, wrap the items in tissue paper, and proudly hand her the bag of purchases with a smile.

"Thank you so much for shopping with us today. I hope you'll come back. I added a twenty percent discount coupon in the bag if you do."

She waves and heads out the door, leaving Lucy and me alone in the store for the first time since earlier today.

Lucy gracefully meanders over next to me behind the counter and bumps me with her shoulder.

"You know how much I appreciate the work you do for the shop, right?"

I turn to the side and wrap my arms around her slender body. While she's about fifteen years older than me and has a family of three at home, we've become good friends. So much so that she's invited me to family dinners at her home regularly. And when I haven't been able to go home for the holidays due to work or school schedules, she's always included me in their family celebrations.

"I know you do, and I'm so grateful for you." I pull back and shift my hip against the counter, noticing how tired she looks today. "Are you feeling okay, Lucy?"

Her form practically slumps from a straightened posture to a weary body stance, shaking her head slowly, as if the weight of it is too heavy.

"Antonio has not been well lately and isn't sleeping through the night. He continues to complain about his tummy hurting. And has had a bad bout of diarrhea." She waves her palm and gives me an apologetic look over the TMI. "Juan and I have an appointment with his pediatrician next Monday."

I reach for her hand, grasping it in mine with a show of compassion. Now I'm really worried about her young son, one of her seven-year-old twin boys, Antonio and Santiago. She also has an older daughter, Maria, who is thirteen.

"Oh, Lucy. I'm so sorry to hear about Antonio. Any time you need me, I'll be there. I'm sure it's nothing, probably just growing pains. But it's better to be safe than sorry."

She nods and presses her thumbs into the bridge of her nose as if to ward off the fear and worry.

"It might not be the right time, but if you want a night out, you're welcome to come out with Christiana and me tonight. We're just hitting up a few bars. Nothing special or crazy."

Lucy smiles a wistful grin and shakes her head. "Thanks for the offer, honey, but I have plans to watch the newest Disney movie and build blanket forts with the boys tonight. But I sure do envy you and your youth. I remember those nights in my early twenties, bar hopping and dancing and doing all sorts of devious things."

Lucy shimmies her breasts and hips, lifting her eyebrows to prove her point.

I choke on my laughter. "I'm not so sure about the devious part, but I do plan on dancing."

I demonstrate my intent by shaking my own hips and arms in a similar fashion, the samba dance move Lucy taught me.

She laughs. "Girl, you're adorable, but you definitely don't have the Latina hip roll. Let me help you out."

She turns on the music of "Señorita" by Camila Cabello and Shawn Mendes on her iPad and schools me on proper dance techniques. By the time I clock out to leave and get ready for tonight, I'm swinging my hips like a pro with the perfect amount of sex appeal and booty-shaking Latin-flavor that I hope will impress my friends.

~

"ARE you sure I look okay in this? I feel so..."

"Hot," Christiana exclaims at the same time that I say, "Conspicuous."

We laugh, looping our arms together as we walk down the sidewalk on our way to meet up with our friends, Taylor and Layla. It's just after ten p.m., the nightlife awakening from its daytime slumber. Music pumps from inside the small bars and restaurants we pass down the block, lines are forming as bouncers check for ID's and collect money from their over-excited patrons.

"You are so going to get lucky tonight," Christiana hoots, giving me two snaps of her fingers and a waggle of her brows with wide eyes as they scan me from head to toe.

I glance down to see what she sees, feeling a burst of proud self-confidence, which I haven't possessed in a long time. Especially with how Miles has treated me lately, with such dispassionate interest, as if I'm inconsequential.

He's definitely not the same guy he was when Melodie was alive. The Miles I knew back then was someone kind, loving toward his sister and grandmother, and an all-around decent guy, even if he was the biggest flirt in town.

Now he's just an arrogant, stuck-up big shot.

At least that was my impression until a few days ago while at the pool, when he acted entirely out of character and became the guy I'd dreamed about as a teenager. The same man I've dreamed about every night since.

Undeniably sexy, charming, flirtatious, and fun to talk to. He was flirting with me, wasn't he?

Now after several very strong drinks at our first stop, while we wait for Taylor and Layla to arrive, my head buzzes happily with the delicious effects of the alcohol. The libations swim through my limbs, clouding my mind just enough so I'm not a hundred percent sure if I'm clearly and accurately recalling what transpired between Miles and me.

What I do know is he's been on my mind nonstop, but it's just a ridiculous fascination and an unrequited attraction. He has no more interest in me now than he did when I was a brace-faced teenager.

Anyway, Miles probably has a girlfriend, and I can't compete with the type of woman he's likely to date. I envision him with stick-thin, sexy models or Ivy League educated, boardroom women who like to get kinky after-hours.

Not someone like me who rarely goes out or knows how to do anything more than study, work, and barely take care of myself.

Christiana orders a bottle of cheap champagne when Taylor and Layla arrive, and we laugh and talk, gaining the attention of a few men who stop by our table to offer us drinks and invitations to dance.

Technically, the offers are for Christiana and Layla more often than not, because they both exude a sensual, exotic beauty that appeals to most men. Both have darker, supple skin, dark eyes with long lashes, and are well endowed.

Whereas Taylor and I are both flat as boards. I may have

a bit more in that area than she does because she's a dancer in a New York dance company and therefore is extremely thin and waif-like.

As I take another sip of champagne, I look down at my chest and sigh.

"What's that disgruntled noise about?" Taylor questions, cocking her head to the side, showing me a toothy grin.

Her long blond hair hangs loose and is down tonight, not in the tight bun I typically see her wear. Her slim nose points downward as she peers at me through her false eyelashes, which she insists are a must-have; otherwise, she has ghost-eyes, with lashes so blond they are barely visible.

I shrug. "Nothing really. I've just never had the same assets they have to attract the admirers like they do."

I gesture with a chin bob to the dance floor where Christiana and Layla dance wildly to an old '80s song, men flocking to their sides like bees swarming around the queen in the hive.

"If that is true, then tell me why the guy by the bar has been watching you the past ten minutes?" She lifts her champagne glass and, using her pinky finger, points toward the bar in the opposite direction of the dance floor where I've been staring.

By focusing on our dancing friends, I've been oblivious to anyone else unless they've been in my field of vision. So, when I turn to catch the gaze of the man in question, I gasp loudly, shock registering across my face.

Snapping back around, I return my attention down at the table.

"Oh my goodness," I mutter under my breath. "I know him."

Taylor leans forward, propping her chin on her hand

and looks to me for an answer. "Really? Do tell. I'd like to get to know him too."

"Mmm-hmm," I absently hum, biting my lip and stealing a furtive glance in my peripheral vision to see if Miles is still looking our way.

He is and something in his molten hot glare is both alarming and hungry. Sinister yet sexy.

There's a moment I think he's going to stand up and walk over to me. At least until I notice the woman that steps up behind him, her arm dangling suggestively over his shoulder, breasts smooshed against his body to whisper in his ear.

A stab of jealousy hits me in the throat, blocking my airway with the intensity of the feeling. Is he here on a date? Is that his girlfriend? And why was he staring at me if he's here with another woman?

None of those questions can be answered at the moment because Layla runs over to our table to grab our hands, drag us to our feet, and pull us out onto the dance floor.

Taylor and I make noises of irritation and utter a few loud curses, but we're soon swallowed up by the crowd and swept up under the lights and the blaring music, as we each unleash our inhibitions and just let loose.

I also let go of the doubts swimming in my head over Miles and his standoffish behavior and allow myself to move and grind to the music.

I lose all track of time, throwing my arms in the air and singing at the top of my lungs with my girlfriends, demonstrating my newly found skills in hip rolls. At some point, I also lose track of Miles, who no longer sits in the spot he occupied earlier.

Disappointment rushes through me, but it's just as well.

Nothing would have come of that anyhow, as it seems he wants nothing more to do with me.

He seems to have other things to occupy his time, and so do I.

Good riddance.

10

Miles

"JUST GET OUT OF HERE, asshole. Both you and your limp dick!"

The door slams loudly in my face, the sound reverberating and echoing in the starless night. I clutch at my wrinkled dress shirt and sling it over my arm, reaching out with my other to steady myself against the closed door, and against the harsh words and the world spinning and turning faster than it ought to.

I'm not sure exactly what happened over the past three hours, but sadly, I'm certain I didn't fulfill my sexual obligations to this woman. My hand instinctively slides down the front of my pants, covering my groin as I cup my cock and balls, confirming that my assumptions are correct.

Whiskey dick did me no favors tonight, which I suppose is the reason my hookup is upset.

It could also be my inflammatory statement about how fake her tits felt and how "uneven and plastic" they were while motorboating said tits. Not my finest hour, folks.

I chuckle to myself out of sheer apologetic humor while I turn around and stare at the landing below. By my drunken estimation, it's a ten-foot drop. To ensure I don't trip and break a leg, I plop down on my ass to scoot down to the bottom. But I get stuck somewhere in the middle and decide I should just lay down because...Goddamn, why is the sidewalk moving? Shoving my shirt under my head, I cuddle up on the hard cement and fall asleep.

A disgruntled male voice jars me awake, and I jolt upright before dropping my head in my hands. Christ almighty, why so loud?

"Yo, buddy. You can't sleep there. Get the hell up and move along, asshole."

My head is the weight of a cinder block. I try raising it, opening my mouth to reply but shutting it just as promptly because I have no idea what to say. No matter, since the guy is already walking away, hand raised in the air, flipping me his middle finger. My body rumbles with laughter, but my tongue is so thick and throat dry, I can't get the sound out.

Having the wherewithal to know I need a ride home, I extract my phone from my pocket, click on the ride app and wait. It claims a driver is three minutes away, meaning I have to sit here and relive this horrible night in my clanging head and wish I could forget it all.

I'll never be able to forget it, no matter how much whiskey I drink because it's my baby sister's birthday. It's a date I never want dismissed or passed over or forgotten. Melodie deserves to be celebrated and remembered every fucking day of every fucking year for as long as I live.

The only problem with celebrating this day is that it

opens the old wound that, for most of the year, hides behind a scar. But it never fully heals. And on what should have been Mel's twenty-fifth birthday, it was reopened and I feel like I'm bleeding out.

When I woke this morning, I had high hopes for the day. I did my usual memorial ceremony in my living room, laying out photos of Mel through the years, her trophies and ribbons, school report cards, and much of the homemade art she'd produced as a kid.

I'd called Granny's nursing home in the afternoon, not only to check in on her rehabilitation and her pain level, but Granny is the only person in the world I could talk to about Mel. Thankfully, Granny said she was fine, recovering well, and she seemed fairly lucid—unlike some days where she doesn't remember who I am.

It disheartened her that I couldn't come to visit her this weekend, as we typically celebrated together, but after the long week I had, I just couldn't do it. I promised I would soon, remaining noncommittal with the timing.

But I could hear it in Granny's tone, her feeble attempt to disguise her disappointment. And it made me feel like shit. Except for Graham, who seems to think I walk on water for some unknown reason, I am shit to anyone else I get close to.

Ask my almost-hookup tonight. She doesn't even know me but knows that I'm an asshole.

A car pulls up to the curb, and the driver opens the passenger window. "You Miles?" he asks, looking a little weary and tired from a Saturday night of picking up drunks.

Nodding, and with some uncoordinated movements, I stand up and climb in the open backseat, my head throbbing with the reminder of all the ways I've failed the ones I've loved.

Closing my eyes for just a moment, I see flashes and images of my life, as if on an old movie reel. Frame by frame, the life I'd had disappearing, leaving just the black film cutting in and out, replacing the good from the past with the misery that has become my daily existence.

"Hey, man, wake up. You're here."

I lift my head and glance out the window, my eyelids half-mast and heavy laden, coming out of what seems like a dream, but is the nightmare of my reality.

"Thanks," I acknowledge, opening and then slamming the car door shut behind me, my brain desperately trying to communicate to my feet that the right foot should go in front of the left as I head toward my apartment building. The night doorman, Frank, sees me struggling and rushes to my side, offering an arm and scooping another behind my back to keep me from falling over.

My eyes roll back and my head bobs like a rag doll when I lift the corner of my mouth in what I think is a smile. "Hey, man."

My speech is slurred, and I'm positive Frank is judging me harshly at my state of disarray.

"Good morning, Mr. Thatcher. Let me help you to your apartment."

I pitch forward and then stumble to the left. Frank hoists me up with his big beefy arms, setting me back on my feet while we stand to wait for the elevator to open.

"Morning?" I'm confused by his statement.

He lets out a low chuckle. "Just after two a.m."

My throat gurgles, and I hiccup loudly. He looks at me wearily. "You okay, sir?"

"Ah yeah, man. S'all good. It was my sister's birthday today," I mumble and slur, drool dripping from my mouth that I wipe with the back of my hand. "Or yesterday now."

Frank props me up against the elevator wall and punches the seventh-floor button. The quick jerk upwards and the gravitational force of being flung through the elevator shaft shifts everything inside my stomach, which churns like a washing machine. I swallow the thick bile that threatens to make an escape, along with all the liquor I drank tonight.

"Looks like you were doing a lot of celebrating with your sister, sir."

His innocent mistake is like a kick in the balls, and I nearly double over from the pain that slices through my entire body, shaking me to the core.

"She's dead. She can't celebrate her fucking birthday anymore."

A protracted pause stifles any further comments from Frank, who I think I've just shut down, as the elevator makes its way to my floor. When the doors open, Frank maneuvers me out into the hallway, my feet dragging in an uncoordinated effort as we pass the Morgan's apartment. My eyes glare at the door, wondering if Sutton is in there. Or if she went home with someone tonight.

The thought irks me.

It should've been me. When I saw her, looking audaciously sexy and sweet I should have bought her a drink. But as usual, I was too late.

"Will you be okay on your own? Can I help you inside your apartment, sir?"

I fish the keys from my pocket and shake my head, turning the key and unlocking the door. I wave him off.

"Nah, thanks, Frank. You're a good man. I can manage from here."

I pat him on the shoulder, and he willingly accepts my statement as truth. He turns and catches the elevator back down to the lobby entrance. But just before the doors close, as I'm still hovering in the entryway, he peers out and says, "I'm sorry for your loss, Mr. Thatcher. Take care."

I sniff at his condolences and fall to the floor in a heap. Like a frigging angry toddler, I bang my fists on the floor and my head back against the doorframe.

It's then I realize sobs have clawed their way out of my chest, tears gushing from my eyes in the most unmasculine display ever. Through the flood of hot tears, I realize this is the first time since Mel's death that I've cried in grief.

And while it's not exactly a relief, it's possibly the closest I've ever gotten to expelling the hurt, shame, and regret I've been holding in for years.

Yet, it's not enough for me to stop regretting who I am, what I've done, and who I've become.

Because that will never happen.

11

Sutton

I RETURNED HOME JUST after one a.m. after sharing a cab with Taylor, who lives with her parents somewhere close. As expected, Christiana and Layla ended up finding *other rides* home, a.k.a. hookups, leaving Taylor and me on our own to get home.

I took Blackie outside so he could relieve himself before we both came back upstairs and got ready for bed. Although I imbibed more than I usually do, I wasn't too buzzed and was actually keyed up, so I took to the couch, turned on the TV, and flipped through some of my social media accounts on my phone. Throughout the night, the girls posted several pictures of our escapades, tagging me in photos of us with shot glasses in hand, smiling, laughing, and dancing. It was a good night, although I ended up coming home alone.

I consider texting the bartender I met a few weeks back

but push the thought aside as I reach out for my glass of water on the coffee table. As I do, I hear a strange, muffled noise coming from the hallway. Blackie, asleep on his bed across the room, growls a low rumble, his ears perking up, but his eyes remaining closed.

"Well, you're a great guard dog," I tease him because that's what you do when you're in an apartment by yourself with only a dog for company.

Throwing off the blanket from my legs, I drop my bare feet to the floor, and quietly shuffle to the door, pressing my ear against it. I hold my breath and listen, as one does when trying to be stealthy to thwart any untoward, unsuspecting hallway intruders.

The sound continues on repeat, this time a little louder. I peer out the peephole but see nothing other than beige hallway walls.

And then I hear it. A male voice, inaudible, but clearly in pain. And clearly a voice belonging to Miles Thatcher.

My fingers fumble to unlatch the three deadbolts. I remember at the last second to punch in the security code before swinging the door open and stepping into the hallway.

"*I'm sorry, I'm sorry, I'm sorry*." His voice shakes and wobbles, as if an old man on his death bed, the sorrow in his words squeezing my heart painfully.

I rush down the hallway, dropping to my knees next to Miles, whose head is bent so far forward in his chest it's hidden in the fold of his legs. Instinctively, I throw my arms around his sunken form, cradling him into my breasts, feeling the sobs racking through his body.

"Miles, you're okay. Whatever it is, you'll be okay." I promise without considering what could cause of this terrible, gut-wrenching sadness.

He shakes his head back and forth, at war with himself, muttering words and phrases that stab me in the heart.

"It's Mel's birthday. I miss my sister." He sobs in my arms for long moments, grief pouring out of him.

As if just now realizing where he is or that he's being held, he raises his head, eyes red-rimmed and barely slits, sweat and tears coating his face and temples. Our eyes meet when he turns his head, and he heaves a sigh—of relief? Gratitude?

Whatever I see in his eyes, it fills me with confidence, knowing I'm giving him what he needs at this moment. Offering him comfort and support in his time of need.

Stretching my legs out in front of me, I prod him with a nudge of my hand to lay his head down in my lap. There's a moment of hesitation, but then Miles complies and finds a comfortable resting place in the cushion of my thighs.

I stroke my hand over his scalp, fingers gently massaging through his dark thick hair, slicking it back from his forehead so I can see the outline of his face. The perfect slope of his nose with a small scar at the bridge and his chiseled jawline that's usually clenched in severe concentration. So far from the Miles I grew up with.

That Miles was a big goof who teased his sister and me mercilessly, keeping us in stitches with laughter. But looking at him now, the outward sadness stapled across his tear-stained face, I see no visual reminders of the boy I used to know. He's either lost his way or hidden away deep inside him. Or, he's just been replaced by a callous, gorgeous stuck-up bastard.

"I know who you are," Miles mumbles accusingly out of the blue, scaring the shit out of me because I thought he'd fallen asleep from the way his breathing had evened out.

My mind reels. Does he finally remember who I am?

That I was part of his sister's life years ago, and by proxy, part of his?

I swallow, the lump lodging in my throat thickly, because I worry that he'll be upset with me that I said nothing before now. That I've been hiding the fact that I know him.

"You do?" I ask, my voice reticent over what he might say.

But what he says doesn't seem to reflect the truth at all. At least, not all of it.

He tries to sit up, pressing one palm to the floor and another on the top of my bare thigh, but seems to think better of it and lays back down with a plop.

"Yeah, you're Ben's cousin. I work with Ben."

Wait, what?

Well, this is surprising and completely unexpected news. I mean, I know Miles is Graham and Soraya's neighbor, but I didn't know he works at Morgan Financial or that he knows my cousin, Ben.

"You work with Ben and Graham?"

He hums a response. "Mmm-hmm. I asked about you."

Curiously, I bend at the waist, peering over to look at his face. Miles's eyes are closed, and there's a little sliver of a smile across his mouth. A thrill flutters in my belly, and I suppress a grin as I press back against the doorframe.

Miles asked about me. What does that mean? Is he interested in me? Does he like me? It feels relatively juvenile, but whatever the reason, Miles was curious enough to want to know about me to ask.

That makes me giddy beyond belief, and I want to know more.

"You did? Why? You don't even like me. You certainly haven't been very nice to me." I can't help but poke him in the shoulder with my finger. He groans and rolls forward.

I nearly jump out of my skin when I feel the barest of touches on my shin, his fingers feathering over my leg and then back down again, tracing a sensuous, invisible pattern.

Holy moly. Miles Thatcher, the boy I used to have the worst crush on, is touching my leg. Caressing my skin. And all I can think about is what if those fingers move further up my leg and press into my center.

Goosebumps break out across my skin, and I clench my thighs together to keep from moaning like a wanton, needy girl.

His fingers absently continue to play, and my legs part infinitesimally on their own accord, as I drop my head back with a quiet moan and a thud.

"I like you," he reveals, fingers stroking gently and so damn delicious. "I'm just an asshole, a prick to everyone. You're not special that way. Believe me, you want to keep your distance."

My body stiffens with anger. "Well, I don't agree with that. You haven't always been such a stuck-up jerk. You used to be nice."

Realizing what I just said, I slap a hand over my mouth to stop any more confessions from slipping out. But it's too late. Miles pushes himself upright and shifts to face me, his expression solemn, eyebrows furrowed as he stares at me.

"How would you know? We only just met. Didn't we?"

My chin drops to my chest, and I screw my eyes shut to hide them from his assessing gaze.

"Sutton," he commands in warning, his voice gravelly and thick from his emotional state and something far more masculine. "What aren't you telling me? Was I right? Do we know each other?"

I open them but keep my eyes downcast, avoiding his judgment. But his finger slips under my chin and brings it up, our gazes locking in silent opposition. Each of us holding firm in our respective corners.

"Tell me."

He may have the upper hand, but I remain resolute, flicking my eyes away, stubbornly refusing to look him in the eye.

"Yes, you're right about me. We grew up together in Mystic. I was Melodie's best friend when we were kids."

"Holy fuck," he bellows. He jabs a finger at me judgmentally, but his voice softens when he says with wonder, "I knew it. You're Button."

I wilt with a feeling of nostalgia as he uses the nickname he'd given me when I was just a kid. Sutton Button. Or just Button for short.

He inspects me, his eyes taking me in from several angles as if he doesn't believe what, or who, he's seeing.

"I knew you were familiar." He slurs drunkenly and even that's done smugly. "Why didn't you ever correct me?"

I shrug my shoulder noncommittally, which his eyes track and follow, the intensity of his glare sending shivers down my spine. In fact, his entire gaze lingers over my skin, sparking flint across the dry surface, until it returns to my face, homing in on my lips. I chew nervously on my bottom lip and swallow.

"I was embarrassed to tell you."

I don't offer more because it would unearth the one memory that I both cherish and want to forget. The day of Mel's funeral when he kissed me and then promptly forgot me.

His palm lands on the outside of my thigh, cupping over the flesh and pressing his fingers firmly into the curve of my hip.

"Why would you be embarrassed to tell me you were friends with Mel?"

I stare at him blankly. Incredulously. Does he not get it? Does he not realize how painful it is to be so invisible to him and so easily forgotten?

I move out of his grasp and work to get to my feet, standing far enough away to give me the distance I need from his touch. From his scrutiny and judgment.

"I'm not ashamed to have been friends with Mel. It's you, Miles." My voice rises, nostrils flare with intensity. Ire. Indignation. "It's the fact that you kissed me seven years ago and have completely thrown it out of your memory. It meant nothing to you. I was just convenient, easy to use, and forgettable."

From the look across his face—eyes wide and dazed and jaw dropped open—it appears my confession has thrown him, and he might be sick. Or that could be the booze. The man smells like a whiskey barrel.

He fumbles to gain his balance, pressing up on his hands and knees and then pushes to a stand, reaching for the doorframe to steady his balance. When he finally straightens to his full height, he clears his throat and looks me over carefully. With reverence.

My body turns from ice to a melted puddle instantly. I back myself against the door, my fingers gripping at the woodwork behind me, digging into the frame to keep myself in place. Miles surveys me like a predator stakes out its prey, inching forward, his body eating up the distance between us until there is no more space.

It's just us and the molecules that circulate between us. The pheromones in our blood bubble and burst like lava, ready to escape the volcano's core. Our breaths mingle in a heated exchange.

Miles moves so quickly I'm not prepared for it, and I gasp aloud. He places one hand over my head, caging me in, while the other cups my jaw, holding me firmly in his hand as he hovers over me.

"Make me remember, Button. Show me how good it felt." His thumb glides softly over my cheek, and I lean into his touch. "I need that. I need something good in my life now."

12

Sutton

THIS MUST BE A DREAM. It's not real. There's no other way to describe it.

Miles. His touch. His voice. The desire reflected in his eyes. Directed at me.

It's utterly reminiscent of what happened between us after Mel's funeral, when I found Miles in her bedroom, sitting in her closet, an open whiskey bottle at his side.

And because I know just how well that turned out for me, I should run. I should make my escape and not allow myself to make that mistake again. I should return to the apartment and shut him out. Leave him to deal with his demons and memories on his own and avoid being just the warm body he uses to ease his pain.

I should do all of that.

But I don't.

Miles has too much pull over me. He always has whether or not he knew it or used it to his advantage.

The sad truth is, I'm just a girl who is secretly in love with him. And no matter how much I want to fight that realization and avoid succumbing to the attraction, I would give anything for one more touch of his lips to mine.

To feel his mouth meld with mine. To moan against the slick sweep of his tongue and feel the heady rush of his warm breath mingling with mine.

I part my lips in invitation, and his hesitation is gone.

He leans forward, the hot press of his body against mine so deliriously decadent it feels unreal. I melt like ice cream in Central Park on a hot summer day.

And then his lips brush against mine, gently testing, tasting, and savoring. But only for a moment, when he rears back, eyes blazing as he stares hungrily at my lips.

"Button," he says again as if reminding himself of who I am and presses his lips to mine once more.

His kiss does crazy things to my body, my brain, and my heart. Taking me on a journey into the past with dizzying effects. Flashes of my youth appear unbidden through my mind: Miles chasing Mel and me around the backyard playing monster, pushing us on the park swing and making us fly high into the clouds and then catching us in his arms as we jumped off.

And then I recall the memory of his senior night party, when he winked at me from across the room, giving me a smile usually reserved for the girls his age. A devilish grin that made every girl giggle with undeniable pleasure to be the object of his affection and only focus.

The memories mix and mingle with the present as I push to my tiptoes and loop my arms behind his neck, opening my mouth wider, moaning when he locks his lips with mine. Miles lets out a cocky chuckle when he pulls back unexpectedly, my arms dropping to my sides, chest rising and falling in fast pants as I try to drag in the air to breathe him in. His hooded lids drink in my face as if committing it to memory.

"You're beautiful, Sutton." He traces a finger over the cushion of my lips where his were just planted, traveling the pattern of my jaw until finally, his open palm encircles my throat.

It's not tight, but it sends a shot of adrenaline through my bloodstream.

Something primal flickers in his eyes, clearly expressing the menu of his sexual appetites. His hand clutches tighter, and he buries his face in my neck, turning my chin to angle my neck away from him as he bites at the sensitive flesh underneath my ear. He sucks and nibbles—sending ripples of pleasure to my tightening nipples—and the sting of pain is both alarming and so incredibly electrifying.

The hard bulge in his pants nudges between my thighs, and his other hand drops between us, fingers skimming the slip of skin exposed between my pajama top and sleep shorts.

Letting out a half moan, half gargled exhale, I punch my hips forward, desperate for his touch.

As if just realizing that we're still in his open doorway, he lifts his head and nudges us inside, tugging me in with the pinch of my waistband. We round the corner, and he slams the door shut with his foot, his hand burrowing underneath the elastic of my shorts, knuckles rubbing over my sensitive flesh.

Miles arches an eyebrow in appreciation. "Beautiful and so fucking sexy. I've wanted to do this to you since the night you made me dinner."

I'm shocked by his admission, but my thoughts are stolen when his lips smash against mine. Simultaneously he runs his tongue through the seam of my lips, shoving his tongue inside my parted lips as his fingers brush through the wetness of my folds.

Holy smokes, this is so much better than any of the teenage fantasies I ever had of Miles. Exceeding every hope and wish I'd made that he would finally kiss me.

Miles is both rough and tender as his fingers graze between the seam of my entrance and flick over my throbbing clit. All this is too much. I'm on sensory overload, between his kisses and his touches, and the compliments he keeps throwing out about how beautiful, sexy, and sweet I am.

"Miles," I cry out, uncertain of what I'm trying to say or ask.

But then all capacity for coherent thought and speech vanishes when he thrusts a finger inside me, curling it to find that perfect spot, and grinds his thumb over my swollen nub. All I can do is moan and sob out a cry of pleasure with long-awaited relief, as my body is racked with the deepest and most intense orgasm I've ever had.

My legs tremble as I come down from the high, releasing a shuddering breath, leaving me bereft as he removes his hand from my shorts. Stepping back, that same cocky smirk affixed to his mouth, he beckons me to his bedroom with the crook of his finger, still glistening with my release.

"Come with me. It's bedtime."

Based on the sultry look in his eyes, I'm pretty sure that bedtime might encompass a lot more of what he just did to me. Miles turns, not waiting for an answer, and weaves slightly down the hallway, removing his clothes along the way.

Unanswered questions that are too big and too difficult to answer right now weave through my mind. Does Miles honestly like me? If I sleep with him tonight, will he remember me tomorrow? What happens then? Will he return to act like the same stuck-up jerk he's been toward me? Or will it be different?

And what would Melodie think if she were still alive about me sleeping with her older brother?

She'd hate it. It's the very reason I never told her about my crush on Miles in the first place because she would've hated me. Mel was the jealous type and would have been upset having to share my attention.

But I'm not a kid anymore, my conscience reminds me. And Mel is gone, leaving only sexy adult Miles waiting for me in his bedroom.

Inhaling a deep breath, I exhale it slowly and make my decision, as I begin my walk down the hallway toward the room where he disappeared. Turning the corner, I hitch my shoulders back in resolve, ready to tell him I can't sleep with him tonight.

There are far too many emotions swirling inside me and having sex with Miles would only create a very uncomfortable situation, seeing as we're neighbors in the short-term. And honestly, he seems pretty out of it, and I'd prefer this happen between us when we're both sober.

But everything I'm about to tell him is a moot point because there, lying face down on his bed, an arm and a leg dangling off the side, is Miles. His jeans are still partially on, with one leg bare and the material bunched at the ankle of his other, and his shirt crumpled on the floor next to him.

Loud snores expel from his lungs, and I stifle my laugh.

This is the man who just gave me a mind-blowing orgasm and kissed me like I was something he wanted more than anything in the world, and not five minutes later, he's passed out on his bed.

I quietly enter his room and walk to the edge of his bed, grabbing the bottom of his jeans and tugging them off. I wait for a second to see if it wakes him, but he's out cold. Nudging his leg back onto the bed, which proves difficult because of how muscular he is, I work to move him away from the edge, so he doesn't roll off in the middle of the night.

As I bend down to pick up his discarded shirt, his arm pops back out and accidentally clocks me in the shoulder. I jump, whipping my head up to see his eyes are still shut, but his lips move slowly.

"I'm sorry, Mel. I'm so fucking sorry."

13

M*iles*

There's hammering going on in my head right now. The pressure and pounding are so painful against my skull, it wouldn't surprise me if someone was using my head for batting practice.

With a low groan, almost too loud for my own ears, I pry my eyelids open, squinting at the ceiling above me. There's some semblance of relief to know I'm in my own bed, but hazy recollections loiter at the outer edge of my mind, leaving lingering questions as to how I got home, who I was with, and what happened.

I'm just thankful I'm home and seem to be in one piece.

The days when I could party until three a.m., sleep until noon the next day, and then do it all over again the next night are long gone. I curse at my stupidity over last night's pity party and overindulgence. Somehow back in college, through the miracle of youth, I could bounce right back the next day with ease and enthusiasm. Now, however, it could very well take days before I'm feeling like my old self again.

I groan, realizing with every breath and tiny movement that I no longer have the constitution or stamina of a twenty-two-year-old. I'm trapped in the body of a thirty-year-old man who forgets what a night of excess and too much Irish whiskey can do to him.

Gingerly rolling to my side, being careful to avoid any sudden movement, I can feel that slow sludge of my hangover seeping through me at every point along the way – my head laden with thick vines, hands sticky from the whiskey residue oozing out of my pores and perspiration, and my mouth a moss-covered pond of thick muck.

My palm presses into the mattress, and I push my body into an upright position, waiting for the telltale signs of hangover nausea to bubble up from the depths of my stomach. Sitting a moment at the edge of the bed gives me the confidence to rise to a standing position, and I immediately regret the decision.

"Oh, fuck," I groan, the contents of my stomach climbing up my esophagus and prepping to evacuate unless I sit back down and stop the world from turning.

My butt lands back down on the bed. I flop to my side, burying my head in the pillow. From this angle, I see my phone and keys on my bedside table beside a glass of water and some pain relief tablets.

Not remembering a thing after leaving my hook up's apartment, I don't know if I was even in a state of mind to pour myself water or not. Did I do that on my own? Something in the recesses of my mind triggers awareness as to someone else being here with me.

Soft moans. Soft voice. Stroking my hair. Telling me it's okay.

The image dissipates from my brain when I peel my lids open again and glance down at my body, seeing that I'm only in a pair of gray briefs. A moment of dread churns through me, because now I remember someone being with me, and I move too fast, spinning my head to peer over my shoulder to confirm.

But I'm alone, and it appears no one else spent the night with me. So it must've been my imagination that conjured a woman to my bedroom.

The problem, however, is that the entire night has been blacked out from my memory. To be honest, it's more than a little disconcerting. I've only ever been this level of blackout drunk once before—the day we laid my baby sister to rest.

I'd gone out last night to commemorate Mel's birthday, and to get away from the quiet somberness of my apartment. I remember sitting at the bar after maybe my second shot when, out of nowhere, a woman sat down next to me and put the moves on me.

I wasn't there to get laid. And the more disinterested I acted, the more the woman persisted. And then I saw Sutton. The sea of people parted momentarily, and when I looked up from my drink, my eyes landed on her. She looked devastatingly beautiful and sexy-as-fuck in a sparkly blue dress that showed off every curve of her body.

I'd planned on going to talk to her. Ask her to dance. Anything, but after another round of whiskey the woman ordered, Sutton disappeared, no longer in my line of sight. So, I'd said, "*fuck it*" and went home with the woman. Did I even get her name? Hell, if I can remember.

Everything else is a hazy clump like a dream that you wake from, catching only fleeting glimpses and images in your head, unable to process everything to make a complete picture.

But somewhere in my foggy brain, I remember seeing Sutton. And it wasn't just at the bar. Was she here?

With a foggy brain, a spasming stomach, and a head full of regret, I finally make my way to the bathroom, relieving myself and jumping in the shower for what I hope will clear away the stench of the whiskey remnants clinging to my skin.

After an hour, or maybe more, seeing as how slow I'm slogging through basic tasks, I'm finally showered and dressed, with coffee brewing in the kitchen as I munch on a piece of dry toast. I open the cupboard to extract a coffee cup, and out of the corner of my eye, I notice a note near a pile of stacked mail on my table.

Curious what it is, because I certainly hadn't put it there, I place the cup down and pick up the folded piece of paper. My name is scrawled in a swirly, frilly script on the outer flap.

Unfolding it, I read it, then reread it, having to grab the back of the kitchen chair to keep myself from falling over.

Dear Miles,

I hope you are feeling better this morning. You were zonked out when I left you in bed. I want you to know how much last night meant to me. And I hope you're not mad about what I told you and that I didn't tell you sooner.

Anyway, thanks for understanding. You know where to find me.

Fondly,

Sutton

Expecting to be foggy-headed and unable to concentrate after a night of heavy boozing is a no brainer. But even after reading Sutton's note several times, I'm still lost as to what she is talking about.

First, what did we do together that meant so much to

her? Shit, did we fuck? And if we did, how do I not remember that? And what was it she told me that I would've been mad about?

Speed walking as fast as I can back to my bedroom, I search for any signs that we may have had sex. I search on the floor, under the bed, and in my bathroom trash bin and find no evidence of a condom. This isn't a foolproof way of confirming that sex didn't happen, but I've always been a stickler for wrapping the goods.

You were drunk out of your mind.

I flip the bird to my conscience and slide down to my butt, my back against the bedframe, holding the note in front of me as if it'll suddenly explain everything, even though it's the fourth time I've read it.

According to my quick assessment, I don't think I had sex with Sutton. That thought brings both relief and a strange sense of letdown, hitting my stomach like a lead balloon.

Regardless, the note also refers to her telling me something. Something that might have upset me. What did she tell me that she hadn't before?

Confusion adds to the constant throb in my hangover addled head, and there are too many thoughts spinning in my brain. I need to find Sutton and figure out what the hell is going on. Because try as I might, I don't remember anything that may have transpired between us last night after I returned home.

And while I may remember none of it, it's clear something happened. And if I want to find out, I will have to extract it from the only other person who might know.

With my mind made up, I finish my coffee, check a few emails, and head over to the apartment next door.

To the woman who seems to be taking up residence in

my daily thoughts and interactions. Who has grabbed hold of something buried deep inside me and shaken it loose, so I'm now unraveling piece-by-piece.

And it feels like Sutton's the only one who can stitch me back together.

14

S*utton*

"HAVE you thought about writing a letter to *Ask Ida* to get her opinion on what you should do?"

I look up from the boxes of clothing that I'm sorting through to find Lucy standing in the doorway, her hand at her crooked hip, pinning me with a pointed look as she snacks on a carrot. We've been recounting the strange encounters I've had recently with Miles, all the bizarre behaviors he's exhibited, and how I finally told him about Mel last night right before he kissed me.

"*Ask Ida*?" I ask, giving her a quizzical glance as I continue to unfold a pile of new blouses from the storeroom. "You mean the advice column in the paper where she doles out advice to readers about their crazy life problems?"

Lucy smiles and gives a rapid nod. "Si. I read it all the time and Ida always gives practical and realistic suggestions, and they usually make me laugh. She's hilarious and tells it like it is. I've wanted to write in several times on how to handle my surly teenager."

I laugh as Lucy rolls her eyes in exasperation over her daughter, Maria.

Returning my attention to the remaining bags of clothing in the box, I consider her suggestion about writing to the advice columnist about my troubles with Miles.

"I don't know. . . I'd worry I'd be identified. That would make matters even worse between Miles and me."

I chew on my lip, sitting back on my heels to consider the possibility of writing my tale of woe to a newspaper columnist to share all my embarrassing moments with Miles. What would I even include in that letter? Would I share everything about our past and history, adding that he's now kissed me twice and each time he's been drunk as a skunk? It makes me sound pathetic and lame.

Lucy kneels down next to me, picking up the box cutter and slicing open another box, this one filled with leather purses and other accessories. Each one of these items will have to be inventoried, by yours truly. I'll iron any wrinkly fabrics before merchandising them out on the shop floor. It's definitely not one of my favorite tasks, but at least I get paid for doing the mind-numbing work. The only problem is it leaves me a ton of time to think about Miles.

"No, you could remain anonymous and change names and the story up a little. Why don't you tell me about the trouble with this neighbor of yours? Maybe I can help you."

My shoulders sag with all the emotion and anxiety I've felt the last two days since the night Miles kissed me.

"Lucy, you have no idea. Everything about this situation makes me feel like a fool. Like a puppy dog chasing after him, desperate for his attention. The only time he's ever paid me any attention is when he's been wasted. The first time was seven years ago, the day of Melodie's funeral. And the other night, it was actually Mel's birthday."

I cover my face with my hands to hide my shame. Just hearing the story alone makes me sound like an idiot. The man doesn't see me as a potential girlfriend or a woman he wants to date. My presence when he's been blitzed out of his mind is merely a convenience when he's desperate.

Lucy makes a *tsking* noise, clucking her tongue, and reaches over to tug my hands free. My palms drop to the tops of my thighs as I open my eyes to see one of her gentle, motherly smiles etched across her mouth, and I can't help but return the smile.

"Sutton, I don't know Miles, but I know the only fool in this scenario is him if he passes you up. You are a beautiful, bright, and genuine young woman who has so much to offer some deserving man. But that is just my opinion. You should definitely write to Ask Ida. She will know what you should do."

Later that evening, after walking Blackie and heating up some spaghetti and meatballs from a frozen dinner, I pull up the *Ask Ida* website on my laptop. Scrolling through pages of previously answered letters, I chuckle out loud at some outrageously funny stories people have sent in and the hilarious responses from Ida. One is from a reader named Stuck-Up Suit in Manhattan. That one is a kind of sweet love story.

Reading a few more letters to get an idea of what details I should include; I open up the "Contact" page on the website and begin typing.

Dear Ida,

I have a problem. I'm in love with my childhood best friend's older brother, who also now happens to be my neighbor. It's a

long story, but the problem is that he barely knows I exist, even though he's kissed me twice in the last seven years. But after each kiss, he's promptly forgotten me. Literally forgotten. He doesn't remember our kisses or even who I am to him. And he certainly doesn't know how I feel about him.

In fact, he's sort of a big shot financial guy and isn't at all like the boy I knew. I know he's grieving over a tremendous loss in his life, and I want more than anything to help him get through it. But I fear it would only hurt me in the long run.

What do I do? Stay away from him or pour my heart out in hopes he'll remember?

–The Forgotten Fool

I stare at the blinking cursor rereading the letter, doing a quick check for typos or grammatical errors before I send it out into the unknown. With a confidence that I don't particularly feel, I confirm the note doesn't offer too many identifying details and press the Send button.

The sound of a door closing down the hallway has me holding my breath and stiffening in my seat. Is that Miles? Where's he been?

It's a Sunday evening, and a glance at the clock on the wall shows it's after ten p.m. I wonder how he's feeling. Was he hung over? Did he get sick last night after I'd left?

Guilt seizes in my belly, gnawing and chewing at my insides like an angry monster, as the memory of me sneaking out of his apartment to return to my guestroom alone haunts me. What I'd really wanted to do was curl up beside Miles and sleep next to him all night.

Yet I chose not to, out of self-preservation more than anything. I just couldn't stay in his bed because I'd end up fussing over him to make sure he was okay as his drunken stupor wore off. And then I'd probably lose all my sensibilities and end up having sex with him.

And that would've been stupid.

The one thing I know to be true about this strange pull I have with Miles is that when he wants to — when that steely, big shot veneer is lifted — he can be effortlessly charming and so damn sweet.

I remember after he and Melodie's mom died, and their stepdad took off, their grandmother moved in with them. Miles was around sixteen at the time, in high school, and he immediately took over as the man of the house. He got the job as a lifeguard in the summer and stocked the grocery store shelves during the school year, working hard to provide for his family.

I never knew hardship like that when I was a kid. My parents were lower-middle class, my dad working at the local fishery, and my mom was an elementary school teacher. As an only child, I never went without anything, albeit we didn't live in the lap of luxury or own multiple cars or anything extravagant. But it was a good home.

Nothing like the home Miles and Mel grew up in. But that didn't stop Miles from always helping others, all while working hard to get himself out of our small town. He achieved in everything he did and got a scholarship to an Ivy League school.

Although I know it was what was best for Miles and his future, it seemed to be the end of the Melodie I'd grown up with. Because as we entered our last year of middle school, that's when our friendship ended.

Over the next few years, I made so many mistakes with avoidable outcomes, that I wish I could go back and change them.

If only that Magic Eightball we'd played with when we were kids could have given us different options, and we'd taken different paths to prevent the inevitable consequences that led us to where we ended up.

An end to a friendship.

A death of a beautiful sweet girl.

And the irrevocable change in a boy as he grew into the man I know today.

15

The Past—Sutton

"Oh my God, Sut. Take this sex quiz with me. You won't believe what boys like girls to do!"

I peer up from the Harry Potter book I've been reading, more than a little shocked and wide-eyed to see Mel across the kitchen table, pointing down at a *Cosmopolitan* magazine in front of her. A magazine far too mature for the likes of us.

I still like reading about the whirlwind romance between Selena Gomez and Justin Bieber. I think they'll totally go the distance and get married someday, but Mel thinks Biebs will break her heart.

I do a quick glance around the room to make sure we're not overheard by anyone, but Melodie's grandmother is out at the store, and Miles just got home from work and jumped in the shower before dinner. One of the primary reasons I've been staying around longer at Mel's every day is so I can get a chance to see Miles.

And when he came home a few minutes ago from his lifeguard job, he was tan, dripping with sweat and was so dang hot I could barely speak. I kept my head down in my book for the majority of the time he was in the kitchen, grabbing a soda and snacks. He'd asked Mel how her day was and where Granny was, and that was that.

But I imagine if he returned right now and overheard us having a conversation about sex, I would die of embarrassment.

"Mel, *shhh*," I reprimand with my finger over my lips to quiet her down. "You shouldn't talk about those things. Especially if your brother might accidentally overhear."

She lets out a cackle of a laugh. "Are you for real right now? Just last week, I caught Miles down in the basement, getting busy with Jessie D'Marco. He couldn't care less if we're talking about S. E. X."

Then she seems to rethink her statement, her expression going from know-it-all to contrite. "Well, he has said he'd kill any boy that tries it with me, though. I guess he has very different opinions on talking versus doing."

Over the years, Mel and I have had conversations about everything under the sun. From how long it takes Princess Leia from *Star Wars* to do her hair. To discussing the crazy antics of the *Wizards of Waverly Place* and how I wanted to meet Selena someday. She's my idol.

Or how we'd try to do our best Hannah Montana southern drawl impression when we talked and played pretend. Or whether aliens on other planets really existed, a topic of serious debate after we'd watched the movie, *Signs*.

We had great times together, always. Until recently, my friendship with Melodie had been rock solid, and we'd stayed safely in the PG-rated zone. While I wasn't a Miss Goodie-Two-Shoes, I was baptized Catholic. This past fall, I'd begun attending weekly catechism classes, receiving loads of religious education and doctrine related to *The Bible*, God's word, and how we as children of God should behave and save ourselves for marriage.

And sex before marriage was most definitely not on the good behavior list.

But over this past summer, I'd begun seeing distinct changes in Melodie. When she was alone with me, she was her same old self. But when we were out in public together, she'd walk and talk differently. Wear tighter and skimpier clothes. And would even curse using the F-word, which she'd never used before.

The day she said it, we'd been sitting on the stoop in front of the library, talking with Lizzie Barrington and Brittany Feldman, and I nearly choked on my Cherry Vanilla ICEE I'd just bought from the 7-Eleven down the street. My jaw dropped at her profanity and use of the F-bomb, incredulous that she said it out loud and in public, no less!

This new incarnation of a more mature and rebellious Melodie was someone I was slowly beginning not to recognize or relate to. But seeing as she was my best friend, I knew I had to stick by her no matter what. I knew her stepdad had been a dick before he left them, and her mother had recently died. Those incidents alone were enough to change a person's heart and demeanor.

I reminded myself that it was just growing pains and a period of change for Mel, and I'd stay by her side and wait it out.

Resigned to acknowledging Mel's question about sex, I close my book, and give her my full attention, propping my elbows on the table and cupping my chin in my hands.

"I'm ready. Tell me all about it."

She giggles and leans in, whispering conspiratorially, "Boys like girls to put their wieners in their mouths and have girls blow on them."

The words themselves are shocking. The image conjured in my head is incomprehensible. I shake my head, narrowing my eyes, and scrunching my face in confusion.

"I don't get it. Blow them like you blow out birthday candles?"

Mel rolls her eyes at my apparent stupidity and pushes back from the table, heading over to the counter to grab two bananas hanging from the fruit rack.

I watch her as she peels back the layers on one before handing it over to me, which I accept with uncertainty. Then she peels the other and stands in front of me to demonstrate.

"Okay, pretend this is a boy's penis." I nod dutifully at this description, glancing between the bananas in our hands before returning my gaze to Mel.

"This is what you do."

As I watch her desecrate the fruit with her mouth and tongue, I wonder to myself why in the world any girl would do this? If this is what sex is supposed to be like, I will never do it.

Aren't boy's private parts dirty and gross? I mean, they hold them when they pee and play with them like they're Lightsabers. This, I know for a fact, after seeing Teddy and Cooper having a sword fight with their wieners when I walked by the boy's bathroom at the *Y* in the third grade. And their penises looked nothing like this banana in my hand.

The banana slides between Mel's lips, gliding in and out, her spittle making the fruit go soft and mushy. But she continues until at the very end, before biting off the tip of the banana and chewing it with a satisfied grin.

"There. Now it's your turn."

How in the world did I get myself into this? It's one thing to watch my friend demonstrate the proper techniques of blowing a banana, but for me to do it too? Geesh, this is getting more and more awkward.

Mel takes my hesitation as defiance and puts one hand on her hip and lets out a haughty huff of irritation.

"Sutton, if you don't learn now, you'll screw it up the first time you're with a boy. You don't want him to tell everyone what a baby you are, do you?"

This is a rhetorical question with a hypothetical boy because I am never planning on doing something like this with anyone. Ever. You can count on that.

I inhale through my nose and release the breath through my mouth, opening it just wide enough to nudge the banana inside, wrapping my lips around the soft but firm substance and sucking awkwardly.

The noise I make has Mel cracking up hysterically, so I add more for show. I moan lewdly, swiping my tongue out and around the fruit, closing my eyes and swirling my hips like I'm playing with a Hula Hoop.

But then out of my peripheral vision, I see Miles standing at the archway into the kitchen, his expression holding absolutely no humor or laughter like his sister's.

With my lips still seated firmly over the banana, my eyes dart to his, where I see a tempest of icy blue ocean swirling in his gaze. His lips part ever-so-slightly before he presses them together and clenches his jaw tight. His nostrils flare, and his heated gaze penetrates through every particle of my body.

The hold I have wrapped around the banana loosens,

and it falls to the ground with a smooshie thud, while I stand still in awkward silence. Miles's face contorts, his features sharp and in warning, as he glances between Mel and me.

His voice is a bark. Tight and angry. "What the fuck are you two doing in here?"

With no warning, he strides in with purposeful steps, bending down to sweep my banana off the ground and then yanking Mel's out of her hand. She is laughing uncontrollably, seemingly giving no shits at being caught doing something so dirty.

"Just go away, Miles. We're only practicing for when the time comes."

Miles disposes of the uneaten fruit in the garbage bin with a curse before spinning back around to glare at us. Mainly at his sister, but with darting glances at me, to ensure I know I'm included in his big brother speech. He steps in close, practically overtaking us with his tall, lean body that smells like fresh clean boy and a dusting of body spray.

I gulp and my body wars with the mixed signals rushing through my bloodstream like a current of electricity. There are zings of elated excitement in places I've only been vaguely aware of down "*there,*" and then there is the crushing pain as if I've been slapped across the cheek, caused by the level of disgust in his tone and harsh words.

"This is not what good girls should do." His voice shakes with vehemence. "What the hell is wrong with you, Mel? Do you want to be known as the town slut?"

Panic washes through me now, a wretched horrifying terror shooting through my veins begging for this to be over, or better yet, never have happened. Wishing Miles never would've walked in on this scene.

No, no, no. This wasn't even my idea. I'm a good girl, not a slut. Neither of us is like that. *Please, I beg of Miles silently. Don't believe this is who we are. We're just kids, playing and pretending we're adults.*

The sound of Mel's defensive, mocking laughter has me nearly jerking away from her. Her face has turned to stone, defiant, and refusing to be reprimanded like this. Refusing to accept the shame her brother pours over us like a waterfall of hypocrisy.

She jabs an angry finger into Miles's T-shirt covered chest. "Don't you dare say that to us. You're the one who was down in the basement last weekend getting lord knows what STD's from that little skank, Jessie. Don't be so damned two-faced, Miles."

Her comment seems to hit a nerve, and Miles steps back as if he's been attacked by a snake, his stern features softening until his whole demeanor changes. Melodie, for her part, stands her ground, crossing her arms over her chest defiantly.

"Fine, I'm sorry. I take the words back. I didn't mean them. I just don't want either of you to do something that could get you hurt. Boys can be stupid and thoughtless. I only want to protect you, Meli."

Using her nickname, and the way his voice softens, seems to do the same thing to Mel's hard exterior. She melts into the hug he gives her as he wraps his long, brawny arms around her and holds her tight.

I swallow and look down at my feet, once again feeling like the invisible third wheel. Melodie and Miles have such a strong sibling connection, made even stronger because they've had only each other to rely on since their mother died.

Realizing they have left me out, Miles opens his arm to me and smiles, nudging his chin for me to join them.

When I do, my heart pounds out a wild beat inside my chest, my breathing turning erratic, as I feel for the first time what it might be like to be loved by Miles.

It's more than comfort and brotherly protection that I want from Miles.

But at my age, I can't possibly put into words just exactly what it is I want from him.

I only know my heart beats for something more.

16

Miles

"MORNING, BEN."

Ben Schilling looks up from his desk with a smile and a warm greeting. Our marketing manager at Morgan Financial is an upstanding guy, but one I haven't had the time to get to know all that well.

"Hey, Miles. How's it going?"

Now that I know he's Sutton's cousin, it gives me all the more reason to chat Ben up to find out more about her—covertly. The woman who has been on my mind for weeks. Who has burrowed under my skin and has me waking in the middle of the night from residual melancholy dreams about my late sister.

I don't know why she evokes those memories.

"Come on in and have a seat. I'm glad you stopped by

this morning because there's an upcoming event I need you to attend in Graham's absence."

Inwardly groaning at having to do something social, I pull out the brown leather desk chair across from Ben and take a seat. I lift my foot and cross a relaxed leg over my knee, unbuttoning my suit jacket.

"What event are you talking about?"

One aspect of Ben's job is to get us out into the community and volunteer to help those in need. The last charity event Ben arranged that I attended with Graham was a thousand-dollar-a-plate auction to raise money for low-income families in the projects.

Ben riffles through some papers on his desk, which looks like an explosion happened because of the mess of files dispersed everywhere. For all the good Ben does, he's a disorganized mess. Definitely not at all how my office looks.

Some might call me a neat freak, but as I've learned, you can really control only a few things in life, and keeping my life organized is one of them.

The one thing I don't mind a little messy and dirty now and again is my sex life. That's when I enjoy letting go, rough and raw.

"Ah, here it is." He hands me a brochure from across the desk, which I accept and give a cursory read through.

When I return my attention to Ben, he continues with a jovial grin.

"We're hosting a volunteer event to help out a local outreach program for troubled youth. You know, kids and teens that have fallen into the cracks of society. Those who have run away from their homes due to abuse or neglect. Some kids have dabbled in drugs, or been sex trafficked, or caught up in gangs."

He frowns in displeasure, and the moment he mentions

abuse and drugs, my body stiffens and my pulse cranks up, my heart pounding like a jackhammer trying to beat out of my chest.

I swallow and nod, hoping to look calm, but Ben seems to notice my physiological change and tilts his head in question.

"Everything okay, Miles? Need some water or something?" He swivels in his chair, opening a mini fridge at the corner of his office to extract a small bottle, handing it to me with concern etched across his forehead.

I accept it gratefully, unscrewing the top and taking a swig, hoping it'll rid me of the wave of dizzy lightheadedness thrumming through my head, a dull buzz in my ears swarms like bees.

This event hits too close to home.

My sister died of an accidental drug overdose ten days before her eighteenth birthday seven years ago.

No one outside of my grandmother and the people in our small town knows anything about Melodie's death, except for Graham, because I was a wreck for a good portion of grad school. And I don't think Ben knows anything about my personal life outside of the office.

As blandly as I can make the sound of my voice, I ask, "What are volunteers expected to do?"

He runs his fingertips over the keyboard and taps away to bring up the information he needs, reading it aloud.

"They will assign volunteers to various tasks, including cooking, cleaning, assisting with art and craft projects, helping with career mentoring, etcetera."

He levels me with his steely gaze. "You'd be an excellent mentor."

I choke out a laugh. "If you say so. I know nothing about kids, though. I'm not exactly the best communicator."

Ben leans back in his chair, dubiously staring at me, his arms crossed over his chest.

"You're kidding me, right? Graham is always remarking how great you are with bringing on new clients, and they rave about your ability to solve problems and clarify the terms of their financial investments."

"Well, yeah," I concur because that is true. I'm damn good at my job and have earned the accolades and praise.

But teens? I couldn't even fucking get the truth from my own teenage sister much less communicate with troubled youth I don't have any relationship with.

I frown. "But this is different. Kids are different."

Ben's quiet for a moment but finally runs a tongue under his front lip and leans forward.

"Listen, Miles. I don't want to make you or anyone else uncomfortable. That's not the point. But these kids, they don't have anyone else. What you're giving them is your time and attention. You'd be connecting with someone who might otherwise be out on the streets, alone and feeling unwanted. Just being there proves you care, and that's what they need."

Well, shit. When he puts it that way, how can I refuse?

Agreeing, I nod and stretch out my hand to shake his. "Fine, you've recruited me. Which, I might add, I'm pretty impressed at how smoothly and easily you roped me in."

Ben chuckles and throws his head back in amusement. When he returns his gaze, and we make eye contact, he asks, "Hey, I didn't mean to dominate this conversation. You came by for something else. What was it you wanted to see me about?"

Suddenly, my mouth dries up, and I reconsider asking Ben anything about Sutton. Does it really matter at this point? What would I even do with that intel? A relationship is out of the question. She's far too young for me, and I'm not interested in starting anything with the demands of my work schedule.

I wouldn't mind hooking up with her, and maybe she'd be open to having a fun, neighborly fuck-buddy arrangement before Graham and Soraya return home from their trip. We could leave it at that, and she'd return to whatever she did before.

I give myself a mental bitch slap because that sounds callous and sordid even to me. But I honestly don't know what it is about her that calls to me. That's why I'm compelled to know more about Sutton.

There's something there that just keeps tugging at me like the edge of a dream. She's familiar. She brings out a long-dormant part of me—and I want to understand it. To either turn it up or turn it off completely.

Biting the bullet, I indulge in my original decision to ask Ben about his cousin.

"There's this weird six-degrees of separation between you, me, and oddly enough, your cousin, Sutton." Ben tips his head, expressing his interest in where I'm going with this. I clear my throat. "She's dog sitting for Graham while he's out of the country. Which puts her right next door to me at the moment. Small world, huh?"

A smile so warm and genuine lights up Ben's face, it makes me wonder if he's in love with his own cousin, as absurd as that might seem. Crazier things have happened, right? If it weren't a thing, then why is there something called "kissing cousins"?

"You know Sutton?" he asks, clearly amused by this knowledge. "Ah, man. Isn't she the greatest? I'm so glad it worked out for her with Graham because she was really freaking out about where she would live or how she would make ends meet for school this fall."

A scowl forms at the edges of my mouth, and my brows furrow. "School? She's still in college?"

I know Sutton is younger than me by a few years, but I have no clue how old she really is. When I first met her, the night of the fire, she looked wide-eyed and young, and I estimated her to be around twenty, maybe twenty-one tops.

Ben shakes his head. "Nah, she's in grad school at NYU. She's almost twenty-five, but it's taken her a little longer to finish her masters. She's been working on and off to supplement her tuition and living expenses. She was crashing on my couch for a while, but I think she wants her own place. I don't blame her. Sleeping on my couch can't be comfortable."

"She doesn't have any other family here in New York?" I ask, prying even further into her family situation, but trying not to sound creepy.

For the life of me, I can't figure out why I'm so vested in learning about Sutton. I remind myself I've just come off an emotionally draining weekend, and it's probably something to do with that. She's the age my baby sister would be if she were still alive. I shouldn't find her remotely interesting or have any feeling for Sutton.

Ben shakes his head. "No, I'm it. Her parents still live in a little seaside town in Connecticut. Since there are no substantial jobs for her to go back to in the summer, she stays in the city."

I'm about to mention that I grew up in a small seaside Connecticut town too and am ready to ask which town when one of his employees pops their head in to ask a question.

Which is my cue to get going. I slip out of the chair,

saying hello to the woman, whose name I don't know, as I walk past her toward the door. Before exiting the office, I turn and wave back to Ben.

"Thanks for your time, Ben. I'll talk to you later this week about the volunteer event. See you later."

And as I walk back to my office, with Sutton at the forefront of my mind, thinking about what I learned about her background, I come to a conclusion.

I will pursue this attraction. Assuming Sutton doesn't slam the door in my face when I ask her out.

17

Sutton

When Ben asked me if I'd be interested in volunteering at Holly's Hope Place, the shelter for troubled teens, I jumped at the chance. Mainly because I want to help kids who have lost their way—either through their own poor decisions or by circumstances beyond their control.

That may sound like an overconfident and self-important life goal, but it's why I'm studying social work and applied psychology. Applying what I've learned in real life, non-clinical settings, is a rewarding experience. You might say I take after my mother in that way.

She's been a teacher and volunteer for various charitable and non-profit organizations over the past twenty-years helping those in need. Whether it's working at a local food bank, reading to young students in a literacy program, or chairing a school supply drive each fall, my mom has always had compassion for others.

And she did the best she could back when Melodie and I were still friends in middle school. She was my rock when our friendship unraveled and dissolved while Mel slowly slipped away, turning into a person I no longer recognized.

There were signs along the way that spoke to the change in Mel, but they were small, and like tiny cracks in the pavement, we didn't see them at the time or understand what they meant. Looking back at what happened, it seems there had been this giant curtain draped over our life, and over the years since. I have peeled the curtain back, giving me glimpses into what was truly going on.

And with each revelation, it breaks my heart even further.

"Hey, Miss Sutton, here's the last of the dishes," calls out Darnessa, the teen girl with a shy smile and the designated kitchen lead. I glance at her as she enters the large industrial kitchen carrying a tub of dirty dinner plates and silverware. "Goddamn, this group is a bunch of pigs and eats a fuck-ton of food."

Elbow deep in dishwater, I wrinkle my nose at the sixteen-year-old and glare at her from under my lashes. "Ahem. What happened to the no cussing rule in the kitchen?"

She provides me with an apologetic look and an "*oops, my bad*" and drops the heavy tub on the counter next to me, filled with precisely as she described, a fuck-ton of dirty dishes.

I splash a cloud of bubbles at her, and she laughs a throaty sound. Working together in the kitchen for the past three hours, I've gotten to know a little bit about this strong and brave girl.

At fourteen, while her mother was behind bars for drug possession, Darnessa lived with her auntie and uncle, a man who ended up raping her and getting her pregnant. After finding out the baby belonged to her husband, the aunt kicked Darnessa out onto the streets, keeping the little baby boy as her own.

Over the last two years, she's been in and out of foster homes and facilities, until she finally found Holly's Hope Place.

Darnessa unloads the larger items and rinses them off as I finish washing the pots and pans used for the dinner we made earlier. I haven't been this exhausted in ages.

"I think this is the last of them, and then we can take a break. But I'm freakin' bummed I didn't get any of that dessert."

Her shoulders rise and fall in defeat over the fact that while we were working our butts off in here, she missed out on the chocolate cake a large box-store bakery donated.

I bump her shoulder playfully and lean in to whisper. "I may have saved us a slice to share."

The look of amazement that lights up her beautiful face made my mission of tracking down a piece worth it in my book. A gift for a gift.

"No way! How'd you do that? Dayum, girl. Are you magic or something?"

My laughter rings out over the pile of dishes. "Not magic. I just begged my cousin, Ben, to save a piece for us, knowing it would go fast."

"Thanks, Miss Sutton. You a'ight."

A bubbly, effervescent feeling takes flight in my stomach from the compliment and warms my heart to hear the appreciation in her statement.

"It's the least I could do. You've been working so hard in

here all afternoon. And you're right. We definitely deserve a break soon."

I reach for the scrub pad while Darnessa empties and then refills the dishwasher as we continue our quest to reach the end of this mess so we can get off our feet for a while.

As we do, Darnessa hums a tune, an R&B song I'm not that familiar with, but that sounds soulful and beautiful with her perfect pitch and voice.

"Wow, that was beautiful. You have a wonderful singing voice. Do you sing publicly, or have you thought about doing something with your talent?"

She turns and gives me a "*what the hell you talking about*" look. "Like what?"

I shrug. "I don't know. Maybe audition for one of those talent search shows. I mean, look at all the singers who have become stars! Carrie Underwood, Jennifer Hudson, Kelly Clarkson. Daughtry."

"Right, 'cause a girl from the projects is gonna get a recording contract."

I stop my washing, removing my wet work gloves, and turn to face her, pressing my hip against the edge of the counter.

"How do you know if you never try? I bet if we google it, we'll find a ton of musicians and celebrities who started off in similar circumstances. Never sell yourself short just because of where you came from or where you are at this moment. You have no idea where life can lead you or the direction it might take if you continue to think positively and with intention."

Darnessa gives me a wary look like she's heard this metaphorical stuff all before and doesn't believe it.

"Listen," I continue, hoping to get my point across

without sounding too preachy. "We all start somewhere, but we all have different jump-off points. It's up to you to decide to step in the right direction. To have the vision and to know where you want to go. Some people create vision boards to enable them to set their intents and path."

Her head pulls back. "A vision board? That sounds like some rich, white girl's bedroom collage, with Zac Efron and The Jonas Brothers plastered all over it."

I laugh out loud at her description because it's kind of spot on. "Okay, whatever you want to call it, the point of it is to tell you where you start and where you want to go."

Picking up a pot, I set it on the edge of the counter to demonstrate, illustrating my point.

"This is your life map, if you will," I point to the pan. "We all have a starting point. And if you set a goal, then you know which road to take."

I place another pan opposite the first and a knife in the middle. But then I remove the second pan, leaving the spot empty. "Without that goal or vision of where you want to go, you'll never know which direction to take or how to get there. And if you never try, you'll never know what you're worth."

Darnessa digests this advice for a second, as I grab the dish towel and finish drying the last of the pots, internally pleased with my pot and pan analogy.

Then she asks in a bored tone, "Can we eat cake now?"

18

Miles

Miles: I'm running behind schedule. Will be there in an hour. Sorry, man.

Ben S.: No worries. Appreciate the heads up. See you when you get here.

Due to an emergency with Granny, I had to head up to Mystic last night and am on the train right now heading back into the city, already two hours late for the volunteer event.

This was not at all how I planned on spending my weekend. But after getting the call yesterday afternoon from Granny's nursing facility, I had to make the trip to discuss her condition with her doctor and then to follow-up with her nursing staff.

Apparently, Granny became agitated yesterday, which is common with dementia patients. But, when the nurse's aide tried giving Granny her meds, she slipped, losing her balance and fell to the ground, reinjuring her ankle and bruising her hip, which was just beginning to heal.

Exhausted and extremely irritated over the situation, I ended up staying overnight in our old house. The house that I still own, even though Granny will never move back in, and I have no reason to keep it. But I haven't sold it just yet. Too many memories exist there, and letting it go would mean letting go of my mom, Granny, and my sister.

And I just can't do that right now.

Granny had been sedated while I was there, and I only had a brief good morning and goodbye conversation with her before returning to the city. She wasn't lucid enough to realize it was me, giving me only a blank, far off stare when I kissed her goodbye.

I've said too many goodbyes in my lifetime. You'd think it'd get easier the more times I've had to say it, but it doesn't. Losing the two closest females in my life, my mom and my sister, and now slowly and painfully losing my grandmother to Alzheimer's, it's no wonder I don't want a relationship with a woman. Why would I want to fall in love and possibly lose her?

It's like knowing exactly how much it'll hurt if you slice your hand with a knife but do it anyway.

Staying at the house brought back too many memories, and I'm in a shitty mood by the time I leave the train station and catch a cab to the youth center. I pay the driver and walk into the old building, the exterior decorated brightly with colorful murals of butterflies, puppies, kids laughing, and fields of flowers with the sunshine above.

It lifts my spirits only slightly, and then they dim again when I walk into the center to find an audience of kids and adults sitting in front of a makeshift stage watching and focusing on a girl belting out a pop tune.

I search the room to locate Ben, hoping to get some direction on what he wants me to do, but don't readily see him. I spot an empty chair in the back of the crowd, so I take a seat and wait until the presentations and songs are over.

The group claps and cheers as the girl finishes her song, and then an older woman steps up on stage and takes the microphone from her hand, thanking and congratulating the girl named Darnessa for her lovely song. She then turns to introduce the next individual.

"Ladies and gentlemen, boys and girls, it's not often we get volunteers who want to get up to share their own stories, but we're honored today to have Miss Sutton join us. She's a student at New York University studying to earn her master's degree in social work, similar to many of your counselors. I can't wait to hear what she has to tell us. Let's give a warm Holly's Hope welcome to Miss Sutton."

My jaw drops open, and my head snaps up the minute I hear her name. I scan the crowd from left to right, in search of Sutton, wondering if my mind is playing tricks on me or whether it really is the same woman.

Sure enough, there she is.

Free from any traces of make-up, her face is clear and marked only with rosy, flushed cheeks. Her hair is pulled back in a high ponytail with flyaway strands making their escape around her ears. She's dressed down, wearing a pair of tight blue jeans and a dark blue T-shirt with the Morgan Financial emblem etched into the front pocket above her heart.

Her smile takes my breath away. She's naturally beautiful, with an inner light so bright that it shines like a spotlight across the room.

I automatically move to the edge of my seat, leaning forward with the need to be closer to Sutton. To listen more attentively. To catch every word that leaves her full, gorgeous lips.

I let out a breath I don't realize I've been holding in as she speaks.

"Hello, Holly's Hope crew! First, let me say I am so proud of you, Darnessa. You took the first step and did it!"

Sutton gives the thumbs-up sign to the girl who'd been on stage to sing. The group erupts in another round of applause until they quiet down again, and Sutton continues.

"Thank you for giving me this opportunity to share my story with you today. I felt compelled to tell you about myself and why I want to go into social work so that I can hopefully work with kids like you someday.

"I had a friend when I was younger. In fact, we were inseparable until we went to high school. It was during our freshman year when I noticed some changes in her. She began changing her appearance, wearing a lot more make-up and different clothing styles that she'd never worn before." She cringes a little, making a funny face that has the kids giggling with laughter.

"But those weren't the only things different about her. She stopped wanting to do things with me, her best friend, and began hanging out with a different crowd. One that I knew based on what I observed and what I heard, were bad influences on her. She started smoking. Stopped doing her assignments. Started skipping school. And eventually, the last year of her life, she stopped going to school altogether."

Although her recounting of this situation could be about anybody, there's a realization that hits me like a bat to the back of my head. It's jarring, shaking loose memories of Melodie during her teen years.

While I had been away at school, first at Yale and then in Philly at Wharton, Granny would fill me on Mel's status during our weekly phone calls. And when I'd learn about her ditching school, or when Granny found a pack of cigarettes in Mel's backpack, I would do my best to imitate the parent she didn't have and discipline my younger sister.

A softball-sized lump forms in the back of my throat and stinging realization forms at the base of my spine.

No, this couldn't be.

There's no way that this woman is the same Sutton that was Melodie's best friend.

An uncanny and remarkable coincidence, but not possible. The girl I once knew as Button was just a cute little girl, not a strikingly beautiful woman.

She continues, "It broke my heart because no matter how hard I tried, I couldn't seem to break down the resistance my friend, Melodie, kept putting up. And what I later found out was that Mel had started using drugs. I don't know the specifics because, unfortunately, we lost touch, and I stopped checking in on her. And to this day, I'm sure there were some clear warning signs, but I failed to see them. And then it was too late, and my best friend died of a heroin overdose. I don't know that I will ever fully forgive myself for not being a better friend to Mel."

The entire room spins, and all I see is red.

Angry, grotesque red blotches cover everything and everyone in my vicinity.

It's as if I've been stuck in reverse over the last seven years, stopped at a red light waiting to move forward, and this is the triggering event that propels me forward.

And all I want to do is yell and hate Sutton for doing this to me.

19

Sutton

"You did great, Sut. I'm so proud of you for sharing that with the kids."

Ben wraps a warm arm around the back of my shoulders and squeezes before giving me a loving peck on the cheek. "I just wish you didn't have to go through that when you were a kid."

"Thanks, Ben. I just felt compelled to share it, you know? It was really cathartic, and had you not invited me, I may not have had the chance to meet these kids. It felt good working with them. In fact, I think I will come back. It's reinvigorated my desire to finish school."

We walk hand-in-hand toward the back of the room as participants fold up their chairs and chat in groups around us. I'm not kidding when I tell him that this day really helped revive my passion for this work, and I can't wait to come back here to volunteer more often.

"Oh, come on. You'd have finished your masters no matter what. Out of the two of us, you always were first in everything. Remember that time when we were kids—"

Ben's sentence is cut off by a booming voice. One I've become all too familiar with recently, but it seems to rattle Ben, who is surprised by the interruption.

"What the fuck do you think you're doing, Sutton?" Miles's voice is ice-cold and accusatory, and he is undoubtedly pissed off. He's visibly shaking and stands in front of me with a menacing, contemptuous glare.

I feel Ben's protective instincts kick in as he steps forward, forcing his way in to create a buffer between Miles and me.

"Miles, hey, man. Not sure what's going on here, but why don't you lower your voice so we can talk about this?"

Ben, ever the people pleaser, places a gentling hand on Miles's shoulder, whose body seems to buzz in protest, his eyes wild and hands fisted tightly at his sides with controlled rage. Over what, I'm not sure? It hadn't even dawned on me that there was a possibility he might be here today. I haven't seen him in days—a week, in fact.

Miles jerks his shoulder away, staring hard at Ben and then pinning me with his riotous blue gaze.

The words he forces through his mouth are *pop, pop, pop*. Like confetti poppers or gunshots. "I. Need. To. Talk. To. You. Now. *Button*."

Oh wow. He went there. Using the nickname he gave me when I was just a kid, because he teased me, saying he thought my name was weird, and that the end of my nose looked like a button.

The memory has me nervously sucking my lip between

my teeth, and I glance at Ben, who is completely out of his depth obviously unaware of what's going on between Miles and me. I've given him no indication that Miles and I know each other or have a shared history together.

Ben's expression holds wary protectiveness, telling me in his gaze that he will gladly do what I want him to do. I scan around the room to see if there's anywhere Miles and I can go for privacy and then decide the kitchen might be empty. Giving Ben a hug and a kiss on the cheek, I tell him, "I'll be fine. I'll call you later."

Turning back to Miles, I tip my chin toward the kitchen. "Come on, Miles. Let's talk in there."

I don't look behind me to see if he follows because I know he will. I pass several people along the way, and Darnessa comes rushing up to me, throwing her arms around me.

"Thank you, Miss Sutton. You gave me the push I needed to sing in front of everyone. Did you like it?"

She steps back, her chin dropping to her chest, looking up from underneath her lashes in a shy gesture.

"Darnessa, I am so proud of you. You were incredible. See? I still have chills from listening to you." I hold out my arm for her to inspect, although truth be told, the goosebumps are from seeing Miles and the uncertainty about why he's so angry with me.

She smiles timidly and shrugs, her toes tapping on the floor excitedly. This would be a picture-perfect moment had it not been marred by Miles's outburst a moment ago.

And I don't want any of that to taint Darnessa's enthusiasm, who seems oblivious to any tension between us.

"Honey, it was all you. But listen, I need to talk to my friend, Miles, here privately for a moment. Can we get together afterward?"

As if she hadn't even noticed him standing behind me, her head snaps up to meet Miles's gaze, who plasters on a polite smile for her, at least.

"I caught the end. You were amazing."

And just like that, Miles turns on the charm, and it's so obvious to see Darnessa melt from the weight of his compliment.

"Thanks," she mutters, cheeks glowing with warmth from his praise. "I'll see you later, Miss Sutton."

She turns and then runs off toward a group of girls, who embrace her with the kind of love and friendship she deserves, as I try to swim through the current of emotions I'm experiencing right now. Pride and happiness mixed with indignation over the way Miles is acting.

I open the swinging door with a bang of my palm and step in the darkened kitchen. A small window above the sink, adorned with a tattered ruffle valance, lets in a small amount of light, but dusk is settling in over the city, and it washes the room in a gray monotone color.

My feet stop in the middle of the room, a center island in front of me, and then spin around quickly to face him. What I don't expect is to find him so close to me, his body hovering over mine. I back up, and my butt hits the counter behind me as he steps forward and invades my space.

His chest heaves, nostrils flare, and we're locked in a staring match. This might be his fight, but I'm not backing down. I did nothing wrong.

"I can't believe how rude you were in front of all those kids," I huff, extending my hand to point toward the room we just exited. "What is it you think I did, Miles? Please, tell me. Enlighten me on how awful I am when all I've tried being is nice to you."

Something flickers across his face—apology? Apathy? Disgust?

He crowds me in but leaves a few inches of breathing space between us. And then he lets loose a torrent of words and emotional baggage.

"Nice? How can you say you've been nice to me when all you've been doing is lying to my face this entire time? *Button.*"

My body jerks in response to his accusation and the heavy emphasis of my nickname. I suppose it should anger me and light me with ire, but it only heats me with something else, and my parted lips squeak out a "*What*?"

"Don't play that innocent game with me. You know what I'm talking about. Button."

He takes a step in, encroaching on what little space we have between us. The scent of his anger is spicy and masculine, with a hint of misery. All that entangles with my irritation and lust that explodes through me like starbursts burning through the sky.

"Stop calling me that," I demand, trying to push him away with my palms on his chest. But he grabs my wrists and locks around me tight. "And I haven't played games. Maybe initially, I didn't say anything."

He sniffs sarcastically. "See? You've known all along who I am. You're the one playing games."

"Miles—" I attempt to subdue him, but he cuts me off, his fingers gripping me tighter.

"No. You don't get to explain. You've had your chance, Sutton. And I don't know what you're getting out of this, but it's juvenile and calculating."

I want to push back and defend myself. To stand my ground and not waiver under his erroneous assumptions. But it would only add fuel to the fire, and from what I've learned in my psychology courses, it's that allowing silence will diffuse the situation faster.

Using that technique, I remain mute, sucking in a breath and exhaling it slowly while my eyelids close to block out my desire to call him out on his arrogance and the misunderstanding of his own doing.

When they reopen, I find Miles's eyelids screwed tightly shut, his lips pinched purposefully as if willing himself to remain in control. He drops my hands and steps back.

When he speaks again, his volume is lower, softer, almost penitent. "Why didn't you tell me you were Button, Mel's best friend?"

I can't help my actions. His question is so desperate and fraught with pain. My hands move on their own accord and cup his jaw with my palms.

His lids pop open to register surprise, looking at me through wet lashes.

"Miles, I told you. Last Saturday night. When I found you on the floor outside of your apartment. I told you who I was and why you thought I was so familiar. It's because I grew up with your sister, right under your nose. But you *never* noticed me. I honestly think you just saw me as an extension of your little sister, and I was invisible to you."

He shakes his head adamantly, refusing to believe my words, but I tip my head in disagreement.

"I know you didn't do it on purpose. I was five years younger, and you were this idol every girl worshipped. And then you left for college, and soon after, my friendship with Mel slowly evaporated, and I disappeared from your lives."

As if it triggers something inside him, Miles snaps his head back, and my hands fall to my sides.

"What you told the group just now. You made it sound like you left Mel when she needed you most."

The festering wound purges open, his pointed words slicing through it like a knife and reopening the wound to bleed out hot and sticky over my soul. It hurts because it's true.

I acknowledge this with a nod. "It's easy to beat yourself up for things you *coulda, woulda, shoulda* done in the past. And believe me, I have. I've blamed myself for not doing enough at the time. But I was a fifteen-year-old girl when my friendship with Mel ended. I tried as best I could to reach her, but she wanted nothing to do with me. And by then, it was too late. I just thought she no longer wanted to be my friend. I had no idea she'd turned to drugs to disguise her pain."

Miles stumbles back, blindly searching for something to hold him up. Finding the edge of a counter, he lays a hand down, his entire body bent and dejected.

"Fuuuck me," he grunts, fisting his hand and banging it down hard into the granite like a gavel, hitting it several times before I rush over to stop him.

When he finally turns his head to look at me, his teary eyes have dried up and are masked with a very different emotion.

Blame and remorse.

"It's not your fault, Sutton. It's all mine. I'm the reason she's dead."

20

Miles

I PACE back and forth in my apartment feeling like a caged lion, predatory and confined, needing to expel the energy and escape. Ready to pounce and tear something apart.

But I don't have anywhere to go.

I know where I'd like to go, but I'm sure she never wants to see me again considering my tirade this afternoon. Honestly, if I'd been in Sutton's shoes, I would have flat out punched me in the balls.

Fuck, I was a complete and utter asshole to her.

And how did she respond to my bullying behavior?

Just like she does everything—with compassion and grace.

Now that I know who she is and how we're connected, I want to know everything about her. I want to know what prompted her to end her relationship with Melodie. What was the straw that broke the proverbial camel's back? Was there an incident I'm not aware of?

The sad truth is that I have no one else to talk to about it. Sutton is the only person on the planet who I can share this with.

Scrambling from my couch, I throw on a pair of sweats and a T-shirt, grab the closest bottle of wine, and head out my door, unconcerned that it's after ten p.m. The thought alone should have me turning around and returning to my apartment, but it only propels me forward until I'm rapping on her door with my knuckles.

I've woken the dog up, as evidenced by the high-pitched bark coming from the other side of the door. Lowering my head, I stare at the ground in front of me as I hear the padding of Sutton's feet across the wood floor and the clicks and clacks of the unlatching of the locks.

"Miles, it's late," she says in greeting. But it's a bit stilted instead of her usual chirpy, cheerful hello that I suddenly miss like a limb.

I hadn't realized how much she's affected me over the last few weeks of bumping into her at every turn. Or maybe it's more than that—a powerful pull from our past, a subconscious spasm of my heartstrings—something I didn't realize contributed to my need for Sutton.

I give her my most charming smile. The one I know has a way of gaining forgiveness from females and one I've shamelessly used various times throughout my life, and the one that I hope grants me an invitation into Graham and Soraya's apartment.

"I come bearing gifts, Button. A peace offering, if you will." I dangle the bottle of wine in front of me through the crack she's left in the doorway.

She plucks it from my hand, peruses the label, and then says, "Thanks," and closes the door in my face.

"W-wait a minute!" I stammer breathlessly. "It's for us to share."

Sutton opens the door again, and this time, I notice her lips twisted in a wicked and playful smirk.

"You little tease."

Her eyes dance with mischief, and she widens the door to invite me in. As I walk into the room, warmly lit with the scent of a candle burning, it fills the space with a sensual fragrant scent of coconut or vanilla. Or maybe that's all Sutton.

She pads into the kitchen, reaching on tiptoes to pull two wine glasses down from the cupboard. Her shorts rise with the movement, giving me a peek of her ass.

Damn it. You did not come over tonight for that, I remind myself, taking a seat on the couch and leaving plenty of room for her to sit.

Sutton's allure is tantalizingly innocent. She doesn't know how tempting and sexy she is without even trying. There's natural confidence infused in her beauty, a rare elegance, and depth that has me itching to peel back the many layers of perfection to find out how dirty she might just be underneath the angelic exterior.

I lean my elbows on my thighs, steepling my fingers in front of me to ensure I keep them to myself and not touch the alluring girl in the room.

When she returns, she sets down the glasses on the coffee table and hands me the wine opener.

"Do you mind opening it? I'm terrible at it. I can never get the entire cork out."

I chuckle and accept the corkscrew, placing the bottle

between my legs and going through the motions as I feel the watchful gaze of Sutton as she stands above me.

"There you go." I hand the bottle back to her and set the cork and opener on the table, waiting while she pours the wine.

Handing me a glass, she lifts hers to her nose. "Mmm. It smells expensive."

"I'd hope so. It cost me a pretty penny."

Swirling the red wine around in the glass to let it breathe, I turn to see Sutton take a giant swig before licking her full lips in a seductive move that has my cock swelling to almost painful proportions. Now I'm imagining her wine-stained lips wrapped around my cock, sucking me deep just like she swallowed that first drink of her wine. As if it's the best thing she's ever tasted.

I clear my throat, sitting back against the couch cushion, and savoring the ambiance.

"You've changed, Miles."

Her statement has my brows furrowing. "Changed?"

Sutton wiggles into the corner of the couch, a good three feet from me. When she twists to face me in a cross-legged posture, my eyes focus on her satiny bare legs. If I were here on a date or post-date nightcap, and if she were any other woman, I would plant my hand on her knee, slowly caress her inner thigh until my fingers nudge under the material of her panties and sink deep inside her wet folds.

But this isn't a date. I don't even know what this is. I'm honestly confused and torn by the pull I feel from her. My voice is rough-edged and throaty when I respond to her comment. "How do you figure?"

She tips her chin innocently, staring into the glass in her hand, as I gaze at the valley between her cleavage. The tank she wears leaves little to the imagination, and the way her taut nipples poke through the material has me wondering if this affects her as much as it does me.

She arches an eyebrow and peers at me over her glass.

"You're just different." She shakes her head and shrugs a shoulder. A shoulder on display that I'd love to sink my teeth into. "You've matured, but it's more than that. You live in a fancy apartment, you dress in expensive suits, you drink pricey bottles of wine. I don't know, you're not the same guy I used to know. And honestly, you've been a jerk to me."

Isn't that the truth? That nice guy she's talking about left the building a long time ago. Taking my heart and soul with him.

But I don't say that.

"I know, and I'm sorry about that. We all grow up and change, Button. It's life. And for me, I've become...well, I guess hard-edged. But look at you. You're barely recognizable from the younger Sutton I remember. You're a gorgeous woman now on the cusp of her life."

I raise my brows salaciously, giving her the barest hint of a smile, my gaze roaming over her chest and body, down to her legs and back up again. My scrutiny seems to have the intended outcome. Goosebumps line her arms, and I notice a flush rise across her neck and cheeks. I raise my wine glass to take another sip.

"You called me beautiful and sexy when you kissed me. Did you mean it, or was it just the liquor talking?"

My hand stops midway to my mouth, lips parted, and mind turning blank. Her question ricochets around in my head like a pinball, knocking it to the corners of my mind before bouncing back and stopping.

I forgot that I meant to ask her what had gone down between us last Saturday night. But I got busy, had to rush out of town, and then didn't see her until today when it was the furthest thing from my mind.

I'm fairly certain we didn't sleep together, but there has been a niggling and hazy memory clinging to the back of my mind. It refused to unveil itself to me, but it's lingered there like a ghost of a touch.

"Sutton, I was not my best self that night. It was Mel's birthday, and I drank so much, I blacked out. I promise that does not happen frequently, but I remember little of what happened. And sadly, it means I don't recall kissing you," I say, and set my wineglass down on the table.

Her face speaks of rejection, and it kills me to have wounded her in this way.

I reach out my hand, placing it on the bend of her knee, the nerve endings in my fingers hyperactive and sensitive to the heat of her skin. Skimming my thumb along the curve of her kneecap, I sweep long strokes over her soft flesh, hoping the touch will reassure her as to how I feel.

"Button, I may not remember the other night, but I can tell you one thing. . ." I stare at her lips for a beat and lick mine in hopeful preparation. "They say a drunken mind speaks a sober heart. And I think you're so fucking beautiful it turns me inside out, whether drunk or sober. There is nothing I want more than to kiss you again."

Leaning forward, I remove her wineglass from her hand and place it next to mine. Then I lift her downcast chin with my finger and peruse her face. I want her to hear and see my conviction.

"The next time I kiss you, Button, I promise it will remain etched in my memory forever."

21

Sutton

When I was thirteen, I'd been walking home from Mel's, passing by the Dairy Queen one hot summer day. I'd babysat the night before and had a couple bucks in my pocket and decided I would treat myself to an ice cream cone.

It had old-fashioned, walk-up "order" and "pick up" windows, so after placing my order, I moved to the pickup window to wait. When I did, some noises from around the corner of the building caught my attention. Being the little Nancy Drew teen investigator that I was, I put on my spy-persona and peered around the old brick facade to find Miles making out with Carli Pfeiffer, one of the DQ employees.

Although there was very little breathing room, Miles held a small vanilla cone between them, one arm perched above her head to prop him up and cage her in. With rapt attention, I watched them as he brought the cone to Carli's mouth and she flicked her tongue out over the top of it, moaning like a dog during a belly rub when her tongue connected with the frosty treat.

I watched as Miles pressed his body flush with hers, flattening Carli against the building, before he swiped his tongue along the cone with hers, and then sealed his mouth against her lips.

My body reacted in a way that I'd learned from my catechism teacher was "lustful" and "ungodly," which immediately filled me with shame. But I couldn't stop the hot tingles that vibrated between my legs unbidden or the envy over Carli, who got that attention from Miles—my unrequited crush.

Apparently, that feeling hasn't changed one bit, only now I'm on the receiving end of Miles's attention. And now I can attest to what Carli must have felt that scorching summer day against the DQ wall.

Miles's hand has stilled on my thigh, his thumb applying pressure as he slides closer to me and leans in to align his mouth to mine. There's a breath of space between us, my chest rising and falling, the scent of spicy red wine and something all Miles lingering there.

"Tell me not to kiss you, Button," Miles rasps, his fingers brushing gently over my cheek before tucking some errant stray hairs behind my ear. "Because once I start, I'm not sure I'll be able to stop."

Holy smokes, is this the type of thing he said to all those girls before me? The ones I would've given anything to have changed places with back then?

And now here I am, my dream is finally coming true, and Miles is telling me not to let him kiss me? Is he crazy?

There's not a chance in hell that will happen.

Wrapping my arms around his neck, I tug him to me, a grunt of satisfaction escaping my throat, filled with the thrill that this time—*this kiss*—will be different. Because this time Miles knows who I am, knows his mind, and his actions aren't being fueled by alcohol or inconsolable grief.

"Kiss me like you mean it, Miles."

His mouth crushes mine, fusing our hearts and souls together in a swirling tempest of passion. I make a strangled noise as liquid heat floods between my legs, a riot of lust zigging and zagging like thrown confetti. Parting my lips with his tongue, he plunges inside, swiping past the seam and into my mouth, running long, languid strokes over my tongue.

We kiss hungrily, eagerly, sucking in each other's moans and groans that rip free from our throats. A hard, dancing pulse flutters inside me, and I close my eyes to the emotion and rapture. I think to myself, *this feels so freaking good.*

Threading my fingers through his hair, I cling desperately to him as my body reacts with eagerness to his kiss, his taste, and his touch. He tastes of wine, and mint, of past and present. He feels like a dream come true.

I'm almost drunk with pleasure from his kiss, when Miles slips a hand underneath my butt, cupping his palm and lifting me off the couch. He shifts back, and my knees sink into the cushion as I straddle him, my breasts practically flaunting themselves in his face.

Miles returns to deepen his kiss as his tongue explores my mouth, darting and toying with me, his hand burrowing underneath the front of my tank top, navigating and surveying the valley of my stomach. Each touch brings white-hot electrical surges to my core. He teases me with the soft strokes of his thumb around my belly, and my body quickly loses patience wanting him to touch me elsewhere.

I grind against the hard ridge in his pants, and he breaks off the kiss with a sexy chuckle.

"Something the matter, Button?"

His smug grin, contoured jawline, and fiery blue eyes appear perfectly calm and unaffected as if he's relaxing on a Central Park bench on a leisurely Sunday afternoon. In fact, without the telltale sign of his erection pressing into my center or his heavier-than-normal breathing, I wouldn't even know I turned him on.

But I'm like a live wire, ready to explode in desperation if he doesn't touch me where I need him to ASAP.

My voice is breathless, and I pant out my demand, "Touch me, Miles. I need you to touch me."

He tips his head back, fingers still gently caressing the sensitive skin above my pelvic bone, looking at me inquisitively.

"Tell me something first, Button. Do you remember that day when I caught you and Mel introducing yourselves to the fine art of blow jobs?"

Like an ice-cold bucket of water thrown over me, I rear back on his lap, my hands falling to his shoulders. That was one of the most humiliating moments of my life—being caught by the boy I crushed on giving a blow job to a banana.

Rolling my eyes to stave off mortification, I return this questioning look.

"Yeah, I do," I demure. "You totally made fun of us and I was mortified you caught us. Why?"

He clears his throat, licking the corner of his mouth, his nostrils flaring slightly. His hips shift, nestling his cock firmly between my legs, as my thighs splay wider to allow more room.

"I probably shouldn't admit this because it'll make me sound like an absolute perv," he admits, the top of his ears turning red.

An embarrassed Miles? Well, this is new and very cute.

I lift an eyebrow, encouraging him to continue.

"I know I scolded you both harshly, but it was out of self-preservation to avoid being caught with the hard on I had for you. When I saw you, your red cherry lips wrapped around that banana, sucking it in and out of your mouth. . . well, let's just say I had fantasies about that every night for the rest of that summer. And because I hated myself for it, I tried my best to ignore you, even though it was very difficult since you were always around."

I think back to that summer, a pang to my heart, recalling the way Miles did exactly that. It tortured me to feel so invisible and overlooked by him. And when we did interact, Miles was overly brotherly.

I pinch my lips together and cross my arms in front of my chest. "Well, at least there's a reason for it, and it makes sense now. But it hurt my sensitive adolescent feelings and really did a number on my self-confidence. It scared me for a long time, and I was afraid to give a blow job to a boy."

A slow, apologetic smile turns up at the corners of his mouth, and he leans in, his lips grazing my ear as he kisses down my neck.

"I'm sorry about that. But I can't say I'm not glad it kept you from getting busy with those stupid teenage boys."

I choke out a laugh, and the confession falls easily from my lips. I peek up at him through my lashes. "It didn't matter, anyway. I didn't have any boyfriends in high school, mainly because no other boy could ever measure up to the only one I ever wanted. But I couldn't have him."

His lips stop at the base of my neck, breath fanning out in a whisper, teasing my sensitive skin.

"Oh yeah? Who was that?"

Placing my hands on his shoulders, I push him back so I can look into his eyes.

Shaking my head incredulously, I ask, "You seriously don't know how bad I crushed on you?"

His blue eyes expand wide in surprise. "You did?"

I give him a mocking eye roll. "Oh my God, you *were* totally oblivious to me. You starred in every one of my teenage fantasies. I waited a long time, hoping you'd finally look twice at me, and you'd be my first."

"I was a stupid, oblivious boy, and I want to apologize to your younger self," he says, bending forward and kissing the tip of my nose. "But maybe there's a way I can make it up to adult Sutton?"

Miles plants his mouth over mine, gently kissing me in ways I'd always dreamed he would. It's surreal he's touching and holding me now, after all the years of wanting and yearning.

But the past or the way he treated me then can't define how I feel about him now.

He's here and wants me now, and teenage Sutton is pretty damn happy by this spectacular and unexpected turn of events.

22

Miles

I DON'T KNOW what I expected when I came knocking on Sutton's door tonight, but it wasn't her ending up in my lap, confessing our teenage fantasies and kissing the fuck out of one another.

It shocks me to know there has always been this connection between us, even back when we were young and didn't understand how hard life can be. When Mel was still alive. If she were here today, what would she think about Sutton and me? Would she want us to be together?

The thought has me reconsidering where this is going tonight. While I would love nothing more than to sink inside Sutton's body and fuck her tonight, I also want to respect the fragile boundaries we've forged within our newly minted status and reunion. She also needs to understand that I'm no longer the guy she believes she once knew.

No, I'm definitely not that guy. He died a long time ago, right along with my sister.

I pull back and lift Sutton off my lap, setting her on the couch next to me. She seems confused as I swing an arm around her shoulder and pull her tenderly into my side. It feels unbelievably natural to hold her in my arms as if we've always been doing it.

I place a kiss on the top of her head, as she snuggles in tighter, raising her legs, so her heels are curled up under her butt.

"Sutton, we need to be clear on something. Or rather, I need to be clear."

The statement has her tilting her head to look up at me inquisitively, her large green-gray orbs staring at me with warmth and unwavering trust.

"What is it?"

"We have a shared history, through Melodie, and that in and of itself binds us together. But just because we have a past, doesn't mean we can have a future. Do you understand what I'm trying to say?"

I watch as her eyes narrow, growing darker in recognition and understanding.

She moves from my hold, staring down at her hands clasped on her lap.

"Not entirely, no. But it sounds like you're getting ready to reject me by implying that you're not the man I need or deserve."

Taking her hand in mine, I thread my fingers through hers and squeeze.

"I want you, Sutton. But that's exactly what I'm trying to say."

I adjust myself so I can look her in the eyes, placing my finger under her chin to lift her gaze to meet mine.

"I like you, and I'm very attracted to you. But I don't date. I don't get involved with women long term, and I am not boyfriend material. I fuck, have a good time, and leave it at that. Button, I already know you are not cut out for no-strings-attached fucking."

In reaction to my words, her fiery spirit kicks in, and she jumps off the couch, creating distance between us. Damn it, I like that hot little temper of hers. I bet she'd be a hellcat in bed.

Sutton turns her contemptuous glare on me. "How dare you, Miles Thatcher. You didn't even realize who I was less than twenty-four hours ago, and now you think you know me and my expectations on relationships and boyfriends, and no-strings-attached sex?"

She huffs, stomping past me toward the door, unlocking and opening it, pointing toward the hallway with a jab of her finger.

"Thanks for mansplaining how *different* we are and how much of a good girl you think I am. I appreciate the reminder of just what an arrogant, conceited ass you are and have always been."

"Button—" I implore.

She raises her hand in protest and interrupts me, "Don't, Miles. Please don't try to placate or bullshit me. I'm tired, and it's been a long day. Let's just call it a night."

God, I've fucked things up again. All I meant to do was ensure she knew what she was getting from me before jumping in. I didn't mean to imply I knew her expectations or her desires for a relationship. But goddamn it, I know that's how it was perceived.

Slowly rising to my feet, I walk toward the door, bending down to pat Blackie on the head when he brushes up against my leg for some attention.

Her posture is stiff, and she'll probably smack me for it, but I lean down and kiss the top of Sutton's head, and then the tip of her nose, and say, "I'm sorry I ruined this. That wasn't my intent."

She exhales sharply. "Intent or not, you made your opinion of me very clear. Goodnight."

Sutton ushers me out with a press of her palm against my back, and if it wasn't such a tense moment, I would've laughed at the boldness of her gesture.

She's such a contradiction. Sweet and generous, as witnessed earlier today in her interactions with the kids at Holly's Hope Place. Smart and witty, as I've discovered in our conversations and from what I've learned of her educational background. But, man, does this girl have pluck.

And now, as I lay in bed, staring at the ceiling rehashing it all, I wish I had Sutton's strength and resolve. She doesn't seem to allow setbacks to break her spirit. She just forges ahead.

Whereas I'm a fucking cowardly robot.

I've been stuck in the same rut for the past seven years, unable to move forward and scared to form any real relationships for fear of losing someone else that I love. But I know I *could* have someone like Sutton in my life if I'd be willing to move from this self-imposed spot and take a step into a new direction.

I'm not sure what's worse at this point.

As I close my eyes, waiting desperately for sleep to come, I picture the image of Sutton floating on her back in the pool. Confidently knowing she wouldn't sink, that she could easily kick and swim to propel herself if she began to drown.

I seem to do the exact opposite. I'm exhausted by all the flailing and treading of water I've done over the years, which only drags me deeper and deeper under the waterline.

The first thing I remember learning in lifeguard training was not to panic, take slow, easy breaths, and conserve energy.

Yet, all I've been doing for the past few years is wasting my time and my energy. Maybe it's time I find a way to do more than just try to keep myself afloat.

Perhaps it's not crazy to believe that my sister may have thrown me a life preserver from heaven when she sent Sutton Fuller back into my life.

23

S*utton*

THE TIMING of *Ask Ida's* response is uncanny.

After waking from a fitful night's sleep and making breakfast for Blackie, I sit down at my laptop to check my email and social media accounts. That's when I see the emailed response.

My heart beats erratically as I click on the message icon to open up the email. I exhale the breath I've been holding in and begin to read, in hopes she'll have some good advice for me on how to handle my strange situation with Miles.

Dear Forgotten Fool,

You'd recently asked what to do with the problem of the man you've known since childhood, a self-absorbed idiot who doesn't remember kissing you. Not once, but twice. Whether it's because of grief or just plain arrogance, one thing is clear. You are not the problem in this situation. He is.

While it's true, he may still grieve over the loss he experienced (and grief is a very individualistic process), you should not feel compelled to help him. And as for how he's treating you with such little regard, to that I say run, honey, run. If I were you, I wouldn't stick around and wait for this man to hurt you again. You're too important and your heart too deserving for the likes of that.

My best advice is to cut your losses now. If it was meant to be, he'll come to that conclusion on his own. Until then, don't be the forgotten fool, but be remembered for respecting yourself and forgetting about him, the real fool in this situation.

Sincerely,

Ida

The letter cuts deep from the blunt truth in her advice. I know I should heed her advice and just let Miles go. Letting him be so I can avoid the feeling of my heart ripping in two, like a massive crack across the Earth's surface.

When I asked Miles to leave last night—okay, kicked him out is more like it—after what was by far the hottest make out session I've ever had, I wondered if I ought to check myself into a mental facility. Because that was all kinds of crazy what I did.

Sadly, the irony is that I was so ready to fall into bed with him.

I've wanted Miles for as long as I can remember, and I'd take him any way I could get him. And I'm not even remotely interested in a boyfriend or starting up a relationship. With one of the hardest parts of my educational endeavor coming up this fall, all I really want is something fun and someone to share the summer with.

And I want Miles.

But he ruined it by making assumptions about me and what he thinks I should want or need. If there's one thing I know about men, it's that if they believe there's a problem to be solved, they dive in to fix it. Apparently, Miles thought I had a problem with just sex.

I finish my coffee and type out a text to Lucy.

Me: Guess what came in my email this morning?

She replies almost instantly.

Lucy: IDK. A discount for a lifetime supply of the little blue pill? Because that's what J gets every day.

I snort loudly, startling Blackie, who lies at my feet, a little ball of white fur curled up under the kitchen table.

As far as summer jobs go, except for the hassle of tracking down Blackie the night of the fire alarm and having to deal with Miles, this has been a pretty great experience. I'm sadly counting down the days when Graham and Soraya return from their trip. It doesn't hurt their apartment is amazing and offers the best amenities of any apartment I've ever been in.

Which reminds me I need to look for another place for the fall, so I don't have to crash with Ben any longer than necessary.

Me: Mmm, not that. But something very titillating for sure. A response from Ask Ida.

Lucy: Ooh. . . tell me everything!

Me: I'll read it to you today during my shift.

I can see her stewing over this, even though we're miles apart.

Lucy: You're a brat for making me wait. But actually, I wanted to remind you that we're taking A in for his appointment today. Please pray for good news.

That's right. Lucy mentioned last week they were taking her son in for an appointment with a physician at the children's hospital. They're going to run tests to see if they can identify the cause of his stomach problems.

Me: Of course. Do you need me to come in early? I'm not doing anything until my shift. Just apartment hunting.

Lucy: No, no. Camilla will open. No rush.

Me: Okay. Well, lots of prayers, and I'll fill you in on the Ask Ida email later after you tell me how the appointment went. Love ya.

Lucy: Gracias. Talk to you soon, *mi amiga*.

I set the phone down on the table and sigh. Lucy has been such a phenomenal boss to me, and subsequently, a good friend. Everything about the way she handles and balances her business, her staff, and her family amazes me. But I know she's worried about her son, Antonio, and I want to be there for her if I can.

I stand and pick up my breakfast dishes, heading toward the kitchen when my phone buzzes again with a text. Assuming it's Lucy once again, I set the dishes down and pick up the phone.

But it's an unknown number.

Unknown: Care for a swim?

I can only assume it's Miles, even though I haven't given him my number. He must have gotten it from Graham, or maybe even Ben.

Staring at the phone, I deliberate whether I should or shouldn't reply. And if I reply, what I should say and do.

But he doesn't give me a chance to answer because there's a knock on the door.

"Sutton? Are you awake?"

Blackie trots to the door, sniffing at the base, wagging his white tail with excitement and then gives a bark of delight.

I give him a mutinous glare. "Traitor."

Miles chuckles on the other side. "I can hear you, ya know."

Much to my chagrin, my eagerness to see Miles beats out my determination to remain grounded in my anger, and I disarm the security systems and open the latches on the door, swinging it open.

Only to come face-to-face with a gigantic floral arrangement. It's so big that it hides Miles's face, which is too bad because I'd really like to see it.

"What's this about?" I ask, peering around the bouquet to see the bluest of blue eyes and a humorous smile, and my heart stupidly speeds up.

"Granny once told me that men do dumbass things that make girls either spitting mad or brokenhearted sad."

The mention of his grandmother has me wondering how she is doing. The last time I saw her was at Melodie's funeral, and then she stopped by my graduation party that spring, in honor of Mel.

The scent of the fragrant flowers does nothing to compare to the tantalizing scent of a freshly showered Miles, which I catch a whiff of as he walks into the apartment, in search of somewhere to put down the bouquet.

Miles finds a spot on the counter, turns back around, and hangs his head in apology. He gives me a sorrowful hangdog look through his thick, dark lashes.

"And then Granny told me that there are only two ways a man can make it up to a woman he's wronged. One is showing up with flowers"—he sweeps his hand back toward the arrangement, and the corner of his mouth curls up in a smug grin—"and the other is through a grand gesture."

"Hmm," I respond, crossing my arms over my chest, the move lifting my breasts, which grabs Miles's attention. His lips part, and his gaze lands on my now pebbled nipples poking through my nightshirt before rising to meet my eyes. "And what grand gesture do you propose?"

I've never in my life seen Miles Thatcher nervous. He was and is the epitome of a confident male. But the slight quake of his voice conveys a very atypical lack of conviction.

"I want to take you out on a date."

"Is there a question there?"

"Oops, yeah, sorry. Definitely out of my comfort zone here. But yes, there is a question in that statement."

Miles takes two steps toward me. His trademark smile—that I know for a fact got him into a dozen different girls' panties in high school—breaks across his face.

"Button," he says, my nickname slipping from his tongue like sweet honey, thick and slow. "Will you go out with me, so I can prove that I'm not an ass all the time and that I can be a decent guy for you?"

He unwraps my arms, his knuckles accidentally brushing over my protruding nipples, causing an unladylike gasp to fall from my lungs. He offers me his hands, which I place mine in and he wraps them up. They're warm and solid, and they tug me closer to him, so we are only a hair's breadth apart. The air between us charges with static electricity, crackling with the intensity of the moment, bringing back that flame that only barely diminished last night.

Miles slips an arm around my back, his palm settling at the base of my spine and presses me into his body, eliminating any remaining space.

"What's your answer, Button? Will you go out with me?"

If I could capture this moment and send it back in time to teenage Sutton, she still wouldn't believe that Miles Thatcher was asking her out on a date.

The gorgeous, most sought-after boy in town, who only a select few were fortunate enough to gain his attention, is asking me out on a date. The girl who was always in his shadow and worshipped him from afar.

I wish I could torment him a little. But that's not my style. I have no desire to play games or make him chase after me. Glancing at the flowers and then back into his dreamy-blue gaze, I tell him the God's honest truth.

"Miles, I've been waiting to hear you ask that question my whole life. Yes, I'll go out with you."

24

Miles

My schedule this week was insane, and by the time Friday rolls around, I'm worn out. But there is light at the end of the tunnel because Sutton had agreed to go out with me on Friday night. The chaos of my job is the only thing that kept me grounded and focused. Otherwise, I would've folded under the temptation to see her every night after work.

The anticipation of my date with Sutton lifts my spirits and propels me toward the finish line. A finish that I hope will lead to a lot more with her.

We'd snuck in time to hang out several times throughout the week before our date, too. A Tuesday morning swim session before work led to a hot make out session where I had Sutton up against the pool wall. My hard dick between her legs, grinding against her like a teenage boy. A cold shower was required for me to get things under control before I left for work.

And last night, our schedules aligned so I could join her and Blackie for an evening walk to the park. I think our goodbye kiss lasted longer than the actual walk.

Which has only increased my need to be inside her. To learn every curve of her body. To kiss and mark her soft, supple skin. To make her mine.

But first, the date.

I've pulled out all the stops for tonight. To ensure that Sutton knows the depth of my feelings for her and how terribly sorry I am for not recognizing her from so long ago. To apologize for the regrets I have for unintentionally overlooking her when we were younger and making her feel insignificant. And most importantly, ask for forgiveness over my recent actions and behaviors.

Yes, I realize I acted like an asshat toward her. What can I say? I don't need a psychiatrist to tell me that the deaths of my mother and sister turned me into the hardened man I am. While their deaths pushed me to become a hard-nosed investment advisor, it certainly hasn't done me any favors in my personal life.

Granny would be ashamed of me, and Mel wouldn't like the man I am now. It's my mission to rectify this with Sutton, replacing the recent me in favor of new memories with the man I believe I can be. Starting tonight.

Tonight, we're at square one. The beginning. With a goal to treat her like a queen, and I am her loyal subject.

Even if I'm no prince, perhaps she'll be able to overturn the frog curse.

~

"Where are you taking me?" Sutton stands at the entryway, not altogether different from the first time I saw her there a few weeks before.

"Is that how you greet your handsome date?"

"Stop. You know you look handsome," she says, with a rosy blush over her cheeks.

"And you look exceptionally hot." I waggle my eyebrows and give her a slow, appraising glance, my eyes tracking her entire body from head to toe.

She's dressed in a form-fitting, black cocktail dress, with bare legs and knock-out high heels that increase her height by a good three inches. She stands with her hands locked on her hips, lips penciled in with the barest shade of cotton-candy pink, hair falling in loose, beachy summer waves over her shoulders.

She is too beautiful for words.

"Have you always been this impatient?" I jest, giving her my arm to take as I escort her toward the elevator.

She shrugs and picks up her purse, raising an eyebrow at me.

As she closes the door behind her, she relays a stern but sweet goodbye to the dog. "Watch the house, Blackie, and be on your best behavior. No getting into the toilet paper rolls again."

Giving her my arm to take to escort her toward the elevator, my laugh escapes unbidden. "TP rolls? What's that all about?"

Sutton lets out a frustrated huff, slips her arm in mine, and shakes her head. "I think my employer conveniently forgot to mention a few things about Blackie. While most of the time, he's a perfect angel, he definitely has a naughty side. I think he was a little mad at me for being away from home more than usual last weekend. When I came home

Saturday night, I found toilet paper strewn all over the apartment floor. It was a complete mess and looked like a fraternity house lawn party."

"Ah, those were the days."

The elevator door dings open as I press my palm in the small of her back, instantly zapped with the same sharp electricity that continues to exist between us. The current continues to intensify and grow stronger and stronger with each passing day.

I punch the button for the lobby and slip my fingers through hers, holding her hand proprietarily. Something I haven't ever done with any woman before her.

She turns and glances at me with a sideways look. "I know what you were like in high school, from what I observed, at least. But what about college? What were you like then?"

"Truth? Or a glossy, classed-up version of it?"

She nudges me in the ribs with an elbow. "The truth, goofball. Always."

I make a *tsking* noise with my tongue between my teeth. "Okay, but don't say I didn't warn you."

"Ooh," she balks, squirming in my hold. "You make it sound like you were a troublemaker. Now I'm really intrigued."

We continue the light banter as we exit the elevator and head out to get into the Uber I'd already ordered before leaving my apartment.

Helping her inside, I watch as she slides gracefully across the seat, smoothing down her skirt as she situates herself in the back of the car.

"I'd say I was a pretty wild the first year. I'd gotten a taste for partying and realized I really liked the freedom of being away from home. And while Granny wasn't ever super strict, there were still things a nineteen-year-old boy couldn't do at home that he got away with in a college dorm."

I stop there, wondering if she'll expect details. Based on the "go-on" expression in her amused eyes, I think she definitely wants more.

"Come on, Button. Do I really need to spell it out?"

She bites down on her lip seductively, her front teeth gnawing at her full bottom lip, and all I can focus on is her delicious mouth. All I want is to capture her mouth with mine and devour her. Take her in the backseat of this car—damn anyone else or privacy. I just want her. I want Sutton more than I've ever wanted another girl. Or rather, woman. Because she is all woman now.

She uses her tongue to swipe over her front teeth coyly, batting her thick dark lashes.

"Yes, Miles. Spell it out for me."

She leans to the side toward me, her knees touching mine, her hand sliding up the inseam of my pant leg until it's just south of my groin, and I have to slap my hand down over hers, capturing it mid-thigh. I hold her hand securely in mine to avoid embarrassing myself.

"Did you fuck lots of girls in college, Miles?" she whispers in my ear, and God help me, I nearly lose it as the crude word spills from her mouth.

Fuck, fuck, fuck.

I'm spellbound as she returns to her spot looking demure and angelic, her hand still caught under my grip, her soft, feminine scent lingering in my space. She just unveiled a new aspect of her I hadn't known up till now, and it's working me into a frenzy of lust with the need to taste her. To fill her. To fuck her blind.

My cock twitches with arousal while her slender fingers toy with the material of my pants. And without further hesitation, I drag her hand to cover my crotch. The pressure of her hand has me drawing in a sharp breath as she exhales a gasp at finding me hard.

That's right, baby. I'm hard for you.

Her passionate, sensual yet uncalculated response to my ardent need pleases me. My dick swells further, throbbing hard with a desire to be touched, sucked, or fucked. Just to see more of her delighted response to this sexy game, I position her hand at the tip and slide it down over the entire length before stroking it back up.

I'm pretty certain this isn't typical first date etiquette, and we may have skipped a few important steps in the *Dating 101* manual. But my cock doesn't give two fucks about the process right now. It simply wants to get to the endgame —with Sutton in my bed and my dick sliding home inside her.

"Sutton," I warn with a ragged breath, my voice riddled with desire. "We shouldn't start something we can't finish."

The caution in my statement is meant to stop her, but it seems to make a case for me.

I'm so hot and hard right now I could combust. Made only worse by the way she's gazing at me, with a mix of eagerness and heavy-lidded desire.

"But what if I want to finish it? Right now?"

I consider my options, because goddamn this Uber ride. I should've had more foresight and ordered a private car with a privacy screen in the back. But who knew we'd be moving this quickly so fast? There has been a tremendous amount of foreplay and build-up between us this week, but I wasn't prepared for this level of intimacy and eagerness with her.

Inhaling deeply, I reluctantly remove her hand and place it back on her lap, swallowing thickly.

"Later." My voice is gruff, but laced with promise, as she sticks her sweet, pink bottom lip out in a sexy pout, like a petulant child.

With imperious demand, not being one to let an act of rebellion go unpunished, I clasp my hand behind her nape, digging my fingertips into her soft, pliant skin and hold her still while my mouth crashes over hers. The kiss is rough, demanding, and more than a little brutal and not anywhere close to sweet. And the loud moan that escapes her lips indicates she likes it.

Through the hold I have around her neck, I feel her heart beating wildly, my thumb covering the fast beating pulse in her jugular that thrums rapidly with excitement.

When I pull back and survey the damage, Sutton's lipstick is smeared, her hair a tangled mess, and her lips swollen and puffy from my hungry kisses.

She smiles dreamily, her eyes flickering appreciatively as she comes out of her haze of lust. My body is strung tight, the pulsing beat of my need welling dangerous and deep in my thickening cock to fuck this girl hard.

Now. Now. Now.

I chastise myself for losing control and sit back to catch my breath. We sit in protracted silence, breaths returning to normal, the air still electric between us.

Sutton's cheekbones tint a rosy, flushed pink as she extracts a small compact mirror and begins adjusting her appearance as I watch the process, clenching my hands in my lap.

"I'm usually more patient than this when I date a guy." She peers at me through her lashes, a humorous glint in her eyes. "But with you, Miles, it's different. I've already been waiting for years, so I've decided I'm not sticking to my three-date rule."

A spike of jealousy hits me square in the chest to think of her dating and sleeping with other men, but my scowl quickly transforms when I realize what she's implying.

I quirk an eyebrow upward. "Three-date rule, huh? Why's that?"

Leaning in again, I nuzzle at her neck gently, where I'd just been rough moments before, skimming lingering wet kisses anywhere I can taste her sweet, fragrant skin. Goosebumps form over the exposed area, and it ratchets up my desire to see where that trail of shivers leads.

Sutton replaces the compact in her purse, carefully laying it back on her lap, setting her hands on top of it in a demure posture before turning toward me.

And with earnest sincerity that I recognize is signature Sutton, she says, "I've wanted to be with you since I was thirteen, Miles. I think I've waited long enough."

25

The Past—Sutton

TURNING thirteen during the summer is both a blessing and a curse.

Once summer begins and school is out, it's hard to have birthday parties with your friends and classmates when everyone leaves town on family trips to the beaches or attends summer camps.

This year is no exception, and because my dad has to work today, my mom takes me and Melodie, and our other friend Sophia, to the ice cream shop on Main Street. I've never liked the texture of cake, but love ice cream of any flavor, so we decide to all go load up on the sundaes topped with sweets and candy, whipped cream topping and cherries. Afterward, we'll return to my house to open presents and then go to the community pool.

This year, however, has given me an unexpected gift that

money could never buy. As the three of us skip arm-and-arm into the shop, giggling because we can't all fit through the doorway at the same time, we unlink our arms to enter. Upon entering, I overhear a group of boys in the back corner of the shop and turn to look. Their boisterous laughter echoes across the parlor.

My eyes scan the area to find where the commotion is coming from, and I see Miles hanging out in a booth with a couple of his pals and a girl who is nestled tightly against him, with his arm slung around her shoulder.

"Oh God, I can't go anywhere without him showing up with his stupid friends," Mel bellyaches over finding her brother here. "He never lets me have any fun when he's around."

We all grab a booth, and my mom heads to the counter to place our orders. I try to look inconspicuous and guardedly watch out of the corner of my eye to see what Miles is doing. Today he's dressed in a faded Zumiez T-shirt, cargo shorts and flip-flops, his dark inky hair a tousled mess that looks ridiculously like Zac Efron from *High School Musical*. And while Mel and Sophia chatter about a boy they met at the mall last night, I can't keep my eyes off Miles.

His easy smile is thrown haphazardly around the table, and all I want more than anything is to be that girl with him right now. The girl nuzzling up to him, basking in his beautiful pretty-boy smile, his arm looped around me, the stories he shares just for me.

And then it happens. I'm so lost in what Miles is doing that the entire building could burn down around me, and I wouldn't take notice. All my attention is on Miles as he pops the girl's sundae cherry into his mouth, pinches his lips together, his lips screwing up tight and moving from side to side until finally he victoriously pulls his masterpiece from his mouth.

I've heard of kids tying knots with cherry stems before. I always thought it was a weird party trick. But witnessing it happen with my own two eyes, as Miles performs it with a sensuality that I never knew existed, it does something spectacularly strange to my body.

There are tingles and fluttering butterflies taking flight in my belly. In fact, I feel kind of sick to my stomach. But not from the flu, or how you feel after gorging on ice cream, but something else. Something brought on by an emotion I've never felt before.

My mouth goes dry, and I swear I have a fever because my temperature skyrockets in a matter of seconds. I cover my cheeks with my hands, and sure enough, they are flushed hot.

"Earth to Sutton! Are you okay?"

Mel waves a hand in front of my blank face, looking concerned over my state of appearance. And then my mom returns with a tray of sundaes and a candle on top of mine.

"Okay, girls, let's all sing 'Happy Birthday' to our birthday girl."

I'm still in a fascinated trance by what I just witnessed Miles do, but return my attention back to my friends, as they sing a very loud, and very offkey, rendition of the celebratory song.

"Make a wish, Sutton," my mom encourages, nodding at the lit candle that flickers with possibilities of wishes coming true. "Go on and blow it out."

I suck in a deep inhale, closing my eyes to gather my thoughts and rally my wish from the recesses of my mind.

There's no need for me to think too hard on what the wish will be because I already know what I want. And when my eyes pop open again, Miles pins me with his gaze from across the room, his lips curling up into a smile so warm I feel it in my soul.

Just as I'm just about to exhale, Miles stands, leaving his group and begins moving with long, confident strides toward my table.

The breath rushes out of me in a burst of air, and the candle is blown out, my friends and my mom clapping excitedly, extolling their birthday wishes for me. But all I care about is the fact that Miles is coming directly toward me.

When he reaches the table, his smile gets wider, as everyone turns to look up at his tall, gorgeous form.

Melodie grumbles, Sophia giggles, my mom says hello, and I stiffen in my seat, petrified that this is some sort of dream and that I'll wake up at any moment.

"Well, looky here. It seems someone is having a birthday party and I wasn't invited." He sticks out his perfect bottom lip in a pout but then smiles knowingly. "Happy birthday, Button."

And then as if it's all happening in slow-motion, Miles bends down and places a chaste kiss on my cheek.

He kissed me!

I can feel the exact spot on my face where his lips touched me, and I lift my hand, lovingly grazing my fingertips over the spot.

Everyone chatters and laughs, but the only thing in my focused orbit is Miles. He stands next to me, his broad body blocking everything else out around him. Miles is saying something, and I can see his lips move, but I feel like I've been turned into stone like we used to play in the game, Statue.

"Honey, Miles asked you a question." My mother's voice

jars me to attention, and I look up at Miles with blinking eyes.

"Huh?"

Teasing laughter rings through the air, and he ruffles my hair. Oh my God, let me die now.

Miles crouches down to his heels, folding his arms over the table, elbows pointing out to the sides. I stare down at his arms and notice all the dark hair running across his forearms, how strong his knuckles are, and the scratch on his upper biceps, barely hidden by the cuff of his T-shirt.

He's so close to me that I can smell the Maraschino cherry on his breath and the sweet scent of whipped cream on his tongue. Once again, I feel oddly dizzy, the way Mel described it when she'd gotten drunk off her grandmother's boxed wine last week.

"I asked you what your plans are for your birthday today? Mel says you'll come by the pool later, and that she's sleeping over at your house tonight. Sounds like a fun day."

"Yeah," I barely squeak out. "Sounds fun."

He chuckles again at how lame I am for repeating what he just said but seems to brush it off when Mel pipes in.

"You should kick everyone out of the pool for her for a little bit and give her a special swim time."

My head snaps to Mel, and I glare at her. She just smiles as if she didn't just set me up. She knows I hate being the center of attention. Even now, with Miles hovering over me, it makes me feel hot and itchy.

Or maybe that's just because it's Miles.

"No."

Miles cocks his head to the side and quirks an eyebrow. "Why not? Sounds like a great idea."

I can't stop myself when I thrust my hand out, and it lands on his arm. "Please don't, Miles. Just don't, okay?"

He seems undeterred by my plea and stands back up, glancing at his group of friends over his shoulder, who are getting ready to leave.

"Listen, I gotta motor. Just wanted to wish you a happy birthday, Button. And I'll catch you all later."

He ruffles my hair one last time before leaving the table. I lift a hand to my hair and rearrange the strands I spent an hour straightening in the first place.

"Your brother is so cute, Melodie." Sophia sighs in the way teen girls do—sappy and with a side of wistful longing.

Mel turns and smacks her on the shoulder. "Eww. Gross. Don't even go there. I love my brother, but he's a player with a side of man whore."

My mom reacts in a mom-toned note of disgruntled reprimand, "Melodie."

Mel doesn't seem to care. She simply shrugs her shoulder. "He is, Mrs. Fuller. He goes through girls like they are bags of Sour Patch candies. And if any of my friends ever thought about him like that, I couldn't be friends with them any longer. It would be just too gross."

My heart deflates like a sagging birthday balloon.

Not that I ever stood a chance with Miles in the first place—because he's five years older than me—and because he obviously only sees me as a little girl. The one he calls Button.

It looks like my birthday wish will never be granted.

26

Sutton

EXCEPT FOR THE hot make out session in the Uber, in which an urge and need so visceral and strong took over me I practically mauled Miles, he has been the perfect gentleman tonight.

But that backseat episode played on repeat in my head throughout our date. And how hard he was for me had my panties wet the entire dinner.

Miles took me to a sushi restaurant—which he'd asked me earlier if I liked, and I said it was my favorite—where we gorged on roll after roll of the most delicious goodness I'd ever tasted. As a poor college student, I rarely get to eat the good stuff. I normally stop by my local bodega where Sam, the grocer, carries a cheap line of pre-made rolls in his refrigerated section. But tonight's feast was five-star phenomenal.

Then we strolled hand-in-hand through the park, beneath a canopy of streetlights and stars and a softly lit backdrop, music spilling over us from musicians and buskers along the path. At one point, we stop by a guitarist, Miles pulling out a fifty-dollar-bill from his wallet, asking him to play my favorite song.

I scrunch my nose in question. "How do you know my favorite song?"

Miles smiles, giving me a knowing cocky grin. "I hear you singing it at the top of your lungs through the walls."

My mouth drops open in alarm. If he could hear me singing, what else could he hear?

The guitarist plays the opening chords for "Treat You Better" by Shawn Mendes as Miles brings our clasped hands up to his chest, pulling me in close as we sway together to the slower version of the pop song.

If the night hadn't already been fantastic and the most memorable date of my life, the swoony moves that Miles has in him cap it off perfectly.

As we dance together in the late summer evening, the sounds of the New York nightlife a distant buzz around us, my head and heart melt, as I remember my birthday wish from long before.

"Can I tell you something?" I ask him timidly, avoiding his gaze by keeping the side of my face smashed up against the rhythm of this heart.

"Of course. Hit me."

My heart pounds out of my chest. "On my thirteenth birthday, I wished for this."

His feet slow to the barest of movement, and he leans back to look down into my eyes. The midnight blue of his gaze is filled with genuine curiosity, along with a trace of humor.

"You wished for a dance in Central Park to a Shawn Mendes tune?"

I give him a look of annoyance. "No. I mean, I wished for you. For you to like me. To see me as someone other than the little Button you always saw me as. I wanted to be one of those girls you kissed back then."

His expression turns serious, and we stop moving altogether, even though the musician still plays the song.

"Sutton, that's adorable you thought of me like that. But I'm glad you weren't one of those girls." He lifts his hands, cupping my jaw in his warm palms. "Sadly, they meant nothing to me and most didn't last longer than a week. I wasn't a good guy back then."

He snorts with self-deprecating humor. "I don't know if I've changed all that much, but I know that if we'd been closer in age, and we had hooked up then, I probably wouldn't have treated you any better. I was a kid on a mission that didn't include loving or being loved."

His thumb brushes over my cheek, barely a whisper. I crane my neck to look into his eyes.

"In truth, Button, I'm glad this thing between us is happening now and not then. I'm ready to treat you right. The way you deserve. Because now I'm able to see how special you really are."

My knees go weak as he crashes his lips to mine, my hands threading through his hair, tugging him and begging him with my kisses to be closer.

The music stops at some point during our kiss, and the busker clears his throat.

"Do you want to hear another?" he asks, looking up from under the brim of his hat, a smirk etched across his mouth.

Miles looks to him and then back at me, his own sly grin sending shivers skittering down my back.

"Nah, man. I think we'll call it a night."

THE MINUTE we get in the elevator and the doors close behind us, Miles is all over me. He slides his palms along my jawline and holds me there as he presses his lips to mine. It's not quick or gentle. It's feverish and an indicator of how things will go once we are in private.

I want to get closer, to feel his body pressed against me —in the spot I need him most. Lifting my leg, I fold it over his hip, his hard shaft nudging at my entrance, as my panties flood with wetness.

Miles groans at the contact and drops his hands to my ass. He lifts me up, carrying me out of the elevator and down the hall the moment the door opens.

As we pass by my apartment door, I wonder if I should check in on Blackie first, but Miles's index finger toys with the lace of my thong, and all thoughts of doggie-duty are postponed for the time being.

Miles opens the front door with a set of keys that magically appeared and swings the door shut behind him with a kick of his heel. Then he spins us around, shoving my back up against the door, our mouths still fused together.

"You want to know what my wish is, Button?" he asks huskily, his lips moving against mine.

"What?"

His fingers sneak underneath the edge of my panties, and he yanks them down, the sound of my gasp escaping my throat.

"My wish is to find out how wet you are," he confesses, jerking the panties off and over my heel as I kick them to the floor. "And find out how sweet your pussy tastes. And then find out how tight you are when you clench around my cock and how loud you get when I bring you to orgasm."

I make a noise of unintelligible gibberish, grinding my pelvis over his hard cock that's now pressed against my bare sex. I speak against his lips. "I say let's grant your wish."

My breasts heave and lift in anticipation, as Miles drops his hand between us and I choke out a sound as he slides a finger through my wet center, a slow and agonizing glide through my folds.

"Ohh," I keen, my head flopping forward into the crook of his neck as I hold on to stave off the need to rock.

There is so much promise of sexual satisfaction engulfed in his deft fingers as they dance over my flesh, teasing me with searing heat until he finally—*finally*—pushes a finger inside, and I cry out.

Our groans mix together in a symphony of sound, relief mingled momentarily until a deep well of need bubbles up for more.

I rock my hips forward, eager for more friction against my clit. He adds a second finger inside me, and his thumb finding the swollen part of my sex, circling over it to launch sparks of pleasure up my spine.

Miles speaks into my hair, biting at my earlobe. "Ah fuck, Button. I knew you'd be so wet for me."

His fingers piston inside me, as a swell of desire courses through my body, tightening and tensing along the way. I take fistfuls of his hair in my hands, squeezing and yanking hard every time the nerve-endings burst with sensation, and he grunts with mutual desire.

Like riding a rollercoaster at the fair, I feel myself edging higher and higher, knowing the top is just within reach. Knowing that while the ride won't last long, the high as I careen down off the top will be amazing and earth-shattering.

"Yes, Miles. There... so close. I'm..."

"That's right, Button. Fuck my fingers. Come all over them."

The filth of his words, the image it conveys, has me spasming hotly, grinding down on his fingers as I soar off the top of that coaster, barreling down with a loud, throaty cry.

Pleasure wreaks havoc over my now weakened state, and I sag heavily in Miles's arms. I throw my limp arms over his shoulders and take slow, shallow breaths in and out of my lungs.

"Miles, holy shit. I've never. . .that was..."

He chuckles smugly. "Mmm-hmm. I know."

As if the world shifted on its axis, Miles swings us around, and he walks us back to his bedroom, which I first entered the night we kissed a few weeks earlier.

The room is dark, save for a small desk lamp in the corner, and as he sets me down on my feet next to the end of his bed, reaching inside his nightstand for a condom, he confirms what I already think I know.

"That was just a warm-up."

27

M*iles*

AFTER GRABBING the condom in preparation of our fucking, I take my time to undress her, with painstakingly slow and careful movements, much to my impatient dick's dismay.

While my throbbing cock screams from inside my pants, I twirl Sutton around, facing her in the opposite direction, my fingers deftly unzipping the back of her dress.

"Did I mention how sexy you looked this evening?" I ask in a low voice, my lips skimming over the flesh of her neck and shoulders, thrilled to see the goosebumps have returned.

Trailing a fingertip down her spine, I hit a roadblock at the lace of her bra clasp, and unhook it, the bra falling to the floor in a *whoosh*. Her dress, however, only peels down to just the flare of her hips. I drag my fingers over the terrain of her svelte curves, her skin a soft, buttery cream that I want to lick and mark and devour in every position.

With a quick pull, the dress loosens and slips to the floor at her feet, exposing the masterpiece of Sutton's backside. I have to count to ten and replay baseball highlights reel in my head to calm myself, so I avoid bending her over the bed and taking her hard and fast from behind.

My cock roars to life, swelling painfully at this thought, pressing angrily against my zipper, straining for friction and release.

With a gentle nudge of my hand against the middle of her back, I bend her forward. Her elbows prop her up on the mattress, her ass raised high in the air. It's utter perfection.

She whips her head over her shoulder, her wide eyes gleaming with excitement.

"I need to examine and ponder what I'll do with my little Button. All grown up now and ready to be fucked."

She exhales a gust of air from her lungs, followed by a sweet little moan as my palms roll over her perfect and supple ass cheeks. Digging my thumbs into the cushiony center, I peel her cheeks open as she sucks in a gasp. Drawing a line down her crease, I play with the sensitive ring as she squirms and writhes.

"Have you ever been fucked back here, Button?"

She jerks forward, alarm evident in her voice. "No, never!"

I chuckle at her response, pulling her hips back to nestle my cock in the crease.

"Relax, Button. I'm just asking. We're not going to do that tonight... not yet anyway."

Oh, but what my devious mind has in store for her. I want her everywhere. My hands roam over the slope of her body, around her shoulders, and then sweep underneath to capture her breasts in my grasp.

Sutton is fucking utter perfection. The weight of her tits in my hands is like holding small, ripe melons that make my mouth water.

I swirl my fingers over the tight rosebuds, circling them and then pinching, eliciting a long moan of pleasure. "Are your nipples sensitive?"

She hums. "Mmm-hmm. Very."

"Good. I like that. Because I'm going to suck them, play with them, and bite them before the night is over."

I continue to plump her breasts, fingering the stiff peaks of her nipples, tweaking and caressing until she's once again punching her hips back and grinding her ass against my erection.

My hands fall from her breasts as I plant open-mouth kisses down her spine while I unbuckle and unzip my pants to free my cock. Dropping my slacks and briefs to the floor, I now stand naked from the waist down, my erection throbbing, desperate to be between Sutton's legs. My thickening dick and sensitive sac want nothing more than to be inside her hot pussy.

"Stand up but face the bed," I demand, my voice thick with lust and gruff from desire.

Sutton pushes off the bed with her hands, and even from the back, I can see how excited she is by the rise and fall of her shoulders and the quick intakes of breath.

Stepping in, I mold my front to her back, looping my arms around her, my cock caught between us, pressed up in the crease of her ass. With one hand squeezing and toying with her breast, the other slinks down over her firm belly and into the juncture between her legs.

Her body is so responsive as she arches into me as if

shaped to fit exactly to my height and dimensions. I kiss a path down her jaw and neck, my hand gliding up the smooth chords of her neck so I can grip underneath her jawline, swiveling her mouth to mine.

My tongue slips between her lips, the heat of her mouth a delicious fire when fused with mine. I slide my finger through her wet folds, her slickness coating my finger as I dip inside to feel her heat.

"Do you want me to fuck you with my cock, Button? To make you come so hard while I slam into you from behind, all while I finger your clit until you're too fevered with need to even stand up on your own?"

She nods, lips parted but wordless. Pulling my finger from her pussy, I bring it to her mouth, drawing her slick heat over her lips and then slip it inside.

Sutton clamps down and sucks. Holy fuck, it's the sexiest, dirtiest thing I've ever seen. The only sight that might be better is if she were on her knees with my cock in her mouth instead.

"You're a naughty little girl hiding beneath this sweet exterior, aren't you, Button?" I tease, pulling my now clean finger out of her mouth and grabbing the condom from the bed.

Fully wrapped and covered, I take my cock in hand, stepping once again behind her. I press her down, so her head lands against the soft mattress, and guide the tip of my cock to her entrance.

I hiss through clenched teeth as a primal, base level instinct explodes within me. Nudging at her opening, I feel the pliant give of her pussy and thrust in with one hard push.

We groan in unison, the tightness of her inner muscles

adjusting and squeezing, creating dizzying effects that have me already seeing stars in my vision.

"Fuck, Button. Do you feel that?"

I'm not exactly sure what "that" is I'm referring to, whether it's strictly the physical feeling of being joined as one, or the deeper connection that's been buzzing around us for weeks. A sense of nostalgia of the past and a clear direction of the future.

I mindlessly move my body, thrusting in and pulling out, the slide of my dick through her deliciously wet folds inciting the provocative sounds of skin slapping skin. The bed moving underneath our weight and the rhythm of the rocking, the pattern of our fucking.

It's almost too much.

I want to be tender and gentle but tear into her until she's quaking so fiercely, she can't stay upright. I want to probe her in places no one has ever touched and be the first man to make her scream in triumph after eliciting more orgasms out of her than anyone else before me.

My intentions are pure, but my desire pure filth.

I want to satiate my thirst with her and scheme to find other dirty means of getting us both off.

I want her bones to be liquid when I'm through with her, as she collapses on the bed filled with my sweat and my cum, satisfied knowing it was me who did it to her.

Pulling out, I flip her over onto her back, scooting her forward on the mattress as I slide back on top of her, sinking in deep once again. This time, I watch her lips part with an O.

My release climbs rapidly, until my hands are white-knuckled, one placed over her head and the other at her hip. Lifting myself over her, I watch her tits bounce every time I slam in and pull back out. And with each punch of my hips, she lets out a sexy gasp of pleasure.

"I want you to come again, Button. I want to watch you come apart and feel you spasm around my cock."

She hums in agreement, eyes closing on their own accord at the sheer overwhelming sensations. I feel it too. And it's so fucking good.

Sutton wraps her legs around my hips, digging her heels into my backside, her fingers clawing at my shoulder blades.

"That's it, Button. Get there, baby."

She keens and thrashes her head back and forth, lips parted and swollen from my kisses.

I feel my orgasm barreling, starting at the base of my spine, my balls tightening with my release, just as I see a wave of pleasure form over Sutton's face, and her legs tighten around me.

"Miles," she screams, as I throw my head back and roar out my orgasm, spilling everything inside her and coming hard and long.

Releasing it all into Sutton with urgency and shameless, shattering relief.

28

S*utton*

Waking to the warmth of Miles's arms wrapped around me, his spicy, musky scent lingering over my body like a salty ocean breeze, is a feeling I couldn't even describe if you paid me.

And leaving this spot of perfect contentment is definitely not on my list of things I want to do. But I have to get back next door to take care of Blackie.

Detangling myself from his cocoon of warmth while trying not to wake him is a task only Ethan in *Mission: Impossible* could conquer, especially at this early morning hour. Finally extracting myself from the sheets, I roll over to the side of the bed, ready to stand up when a hand clasps around my wrist, tugging me back, my breath hitching out in surprise.

"Just where do you think you're sneaking off to this

morning?"

I give him a sidelong glance to see that smile playing across his lips before his mouth attaches to my exposed arm, kissing a light, tantalizing trail of kisses down to my elbow. I then find myself flipped on my back, facing the ceiling through some ninja move as he begins lazily sucking on a nipple between his teeth. I try to suppress the tremor that runs through me, but my defenses are useless against his sexual warfare.

The things he did last night to me—hallelujah, praise Jesus—were meant to bring a woman to her knees and wave a white flag of surrender.

The scrape of his beard tickles my sensitive flesh, flashing a lightning-fast arousal between my legs, which open to him on their own accord.

"Miles, I have to go," I say half-heartedly, offering up a paltry attempt to escape while I thread my fingers through his messy bedhead hair and whimper. "Blackie needs me."

He peers up at me, one thick brow quirked, his blue eyes the color of the ocean this morning.

"I need you, Button. One more time before I let you out of my bed."

How the heck do I resist when Miles scoots down my already flushed body, his lips working their way past my ignored protests until he reaches my core. His hands coast over the curves of my body, finally taking up residence between my thighs, his fingertips curling around the meaty flesh, parting me wide. Something hot and tight clenches low in my belly the minute he licks a swath over my belly button, tracing an invisible line down to my clit.

With the first flick of his tongue over my swollen nub, I know it's useless, and I writhe under his focused ministrations in defeat.

His fingers part my folds, and the tip of his tongue breeches my entrance, slipping inside with devastating skill and practice.

His skillful talents render me speechless, murmuring only unintelligible words or lusty moans with every lash of his tongue or slide of his fingers.

While my sexual experience is limited to three men, one of which was a fairly drunken and fumbling hookup in the bathroom of a fraternity house my sophomore year in college, it goes without saying that Miles has far more expertise in this area.

Especially given how easily he can turn me into a limp and completely biddable bed partner.

Miles's head pops up, his eyes scanning my face. "Don't tell me you're still worried about the dog. He's fine, Button. We let him out late last night, he's fine for a little while longer."

I prop myself up on my elbows and stare down at Miles over my breasts tinged pink from the scrape of his stubble, his gorgeous body splayed out between my legs. His own legs dangle off the end of the bed, the perfect bubble of his butt visible from my vantage point.

My God, this all feels so surreal. An unbelievable twist of fate that normally would have only been in my dreams.

"I'm not worried. I'm perfectly happy."

He swipes the back of his hand over his wet mouth, covered in my essence, and he grins.

"Glad to hear it. Let's see if I can extend that happiness a bit further, shall we?"

And then he returns his face between my legs and continues to do just that.

Making me a very happy and satisfied woman, one orgasm at a time.

"HEY, I have an idea if you're open to it," Miles says from beside me in the kitchen where we finish cleaning up the breakfast dishes, bellies full and Blackie's needs attended to after that amazing round of morning sex.

I reach up, standing on my tiptoes to return a plate into the cupboard and feel the curl of his hands as they circle around my waist, hoisting me up and then setting me back down. I peer over my shoulder at him, my eyes lighting with piqued interest.

"What idea is that?"

Miles spins me around to face him, returning his palms to my lower back, just above the curve of my ass and tugs me in close. I crane my neck back to look into his face, seeing a new, unexpected expression.

The affection in his eyes projects contentment, which is the first time I've seen it since our reunion. It gives me pause, thrilled to know that I might be the reason for that, but also curious whether it's the aftereffect of sex hormones.

"I know you have to work for a few hours today to open the shop, but maybe afterward, we can pick up lunch and head back home to see Granny."

The shock on my face is probably evident, my eyebrows raised in surprise.

"Really?" I can't contain the smile that erupts on my lips as I throw my arms around Miles and jump up and down like a kid on Christmas. "That would make me so happy to see her. It's been so long. . . since–" I stop abruptly, noticing the dimming of Miles's eyes that grow dark with grief, shaded by loss.

I shake my head. "I'm sorry, Miles. I know it's uncomfortable for you to talk about Melodie's funeral."

He closes his eyes, agony etched over his brow line, and a prolonged silence falls over us. Melodie's life and death have seemed to be an off-limit topic in conversing with Miles, so I've treaded carefully, avoiding that landmine and staying on relatively safer subjects.

But I walked right into this one when he mentioned his grandmother. A woman I knew and loved as a kid, and the woman who raised Miles and Mel after their mother died.

The shutters seem to lift as Miles opens his eyes, and his compressed lips part slightly, signifying his resolve.

He strokes my jawline with a soft brush of his thumb, as if memorizing the structure of my face and the pattern of my skin.

"It's fine, Button. It's still hard for me to discuss Mel's death or even think about it. But I don't want you to walk on eggshells, either. I think it would be fun for us to go back home, hang out with Granny for a bit, and do something fun in our hometown. When was the last time you were home?"

His question hits me with a measure of guilt, and my shoulders fall. "I went home to see my parents right after school ended in May. I've been so busy since then, and this dog sitting job came out of the blue. I haven't been home again this summer."

He pops my nose with his index finger and nods. "Okay then. We'll kill two birds with one stone this weekend. Let's plan on leaving the city by three. I'll get a car and pick you up at your shop, and then we can make it in time to have dinner with Granny."

"That sounds like a perfect plan."

29

Miles

I RENT a car from a local shop and pick up Sutton in front of the boutique in SoHo before we get out on the open road.

Once you navigate through the chaotic and slow city traffic and make it out of town, the drive back home to Mystic isn't too bad of a journey. The further and further we get out of city limits, the less traffic we find on the road.

The satellite radio station plays some music we're not really paying any attention to. Blackie is sleeping in the back seat on his blanket. Sutton and I chat comfortably together, an easy conversation that is both fun and enlightening. We're playing a little game called Truth or Dare. Although, the dares are limited to what can be done in the car.

It's her turn to ask a question. She thinks about it briefly and then snaps her fingers.

"I know," she enthuses. "Have you ever been given road head?"

I nearly swerve off the road, my head snapping to hers to see her naughty smile and tongue sweeping over her front teeth.

I answer truthfully. "No, not while driving. In a car, yes."

There's a slight pause, and I realize she's waiting for me to ask in return.

"Truth or dare. Have you ever given road head, Sutton?"

That's all it takes for the interior of the car to heat up, and I reach over to lower the car's temperature. I take a moment to glance at her, as she leans over the console, her hand landing in my lap.

My foot jerks down slightly with a punch to the gas, and she giggles.

"Miles, do I make you nervous?"

I clear my throat. "Answer the question. Truth or dare?"

I glance down to see her hand grazing up my thigh, toward the bulge that has already formed between my legs, my hard on turning impossibly uncomfortable.

"Dare me, Miles."

"Fuck," I groan through gritted teeth. "You're killing me here, Button."

Her nimble fingers get to my pants, unsnapping and then unzipping them, the sound of the zipper marking a momentous moment.

She slips her hand down my shorts and pulls my throbbing cock out, unable to expose the entire root due to space constraints. Glancing down at my lap, I can see her hand clasped tightly at the base, nudging the material out of the way, and pre-cum glistening over the tip.

And then she goes in for the kill, working to shift her body through the restraints of the safety belt.

"Keep your eyes on the road," she says and leans over so her mouth covers my cock.

I groan, dropping my hand to the top of her head, her hair fanning out to cover her face. I sweep it back in my fist, mostly so I can watch myself fuck her mouth.

She wraps her lips around me and twirls the tip of her tongue over the head, and just that bit of warmth has me nearly losing it right there. I grit my teeth in agony, or painful pleasure, working to stave off an orgasm that I'm seconds away from having.

"That's right, baby. Take all of me, Button. Swallow me down."

I can't help talking dirty to Sutton. She seems to love it and moans around my cock as I swell even further in her mouth.

She flattens her tongue, licking and swirling the turgid flesh of my erection before she sucks me back down. Each time I hit the back of her throat, my hips punching upwards, she chokes and gags a little, and I get impossibly harder. But I wouldn't have her stop for anything.

How I'm able to keep my attention on the road is beyond me. But it's not even a minute later, when my clasp on her hair tightens, and the pleasure crashes over me, my release shooting hot and hard inside her mouth.

She swipes her hand across her mouth after she pulls off, and I just stare at her in disbelief, still panting from my climax.

I tuck myself back inside my pants, feeling the post-orgasm satisfaction sweep over me. Sutton adjusts herself back in her seat, smiling proudly when she says, "There. Now I can say I've given road head."

We continue traveling north east along Interstate 95, through smaller, privileged commuter towns like Darien and Stamford, until we pass New Haven, the home of my alma mater, Yale University.

As we do, Sutton asks, "Do you remember the time when Mel and I snuck out and showed up unannounced on campus?"

Our hands are clasped together over the center console and I bring her hand to my lips, brushing a kiss over her knuckles, recalling the exact memory she's referring to.

"As a matter of fact, I do. I had no idea what I was going to do with two fifteen-year-old girls in my dorm room for the night. I was so pissed at Mel that weekend. She was such a handful."

A heavy silence falls over us as I remember bits and pieces of that weekend years before. Mel had always had a stubborn streak, made worse after our mother's death and all the changes that occurred as she hit puberty. It was during that time when I left for school an hour away, turning my back on my younger sister who needed guidance and structure, love, and protection.

Sutton gives my hand a shake, pulling me out of my reverie. "Hey, you okay? Is it okay to talk about this?"

I smile tightly. "Of course. Thank God for you, Button, because at least you tried steering Mel in the right direction."

Out of the corner of my eye, I see Sutton's head turn to stare out the window, watching groves of trees, lampposts and mile marker signs whiz by along the highway.

"I didn't do a very good job of it."

Tugging her hand so she snaps toward me, I give her a curt head shake. "We are not doing this today. We are not feeling sorry for ourselves. We already talked through this, and you have nothing to be ashamed about. Mel had issues. Deep, hurting pain that she chose to deal with in her own headstrong way. Honestly, I noticed it that weekend but chose to ignore it, unable as a twenty-one-year-old to manage my own teenage sister. I thought she was just acting out and being a brat full of rebellious teen angst. But you, Button. You were the angel on her shoulder."

Sutton gives me a half-hearted smile and then, as if shaking off the melancholy, pipes up with her own memory.

"That weekend was the first time I'd ever gotten drunk."

"Glad to know I was such a good influence," I snort. "I do remember you puking your guts out in my toilet that night."

And then a look of horror strikes across her face, her hand flying to her lips to cover her open mouth.

"Oh my God, I think I told you my secret that night. Do you remember?"

Chuckling, because I do vaguely recall her spilling the beans, I shrug innocently. "I'll never tell."

She bats at my chest, and I duck out of her way, laughing with mirth but grab her hand and hold it in my grasp once again.

"I think you may have mentioned you'd never been kissed by a boy, and you'd wanted me to kiss you."

Sutton's head hangs down between her shoulders like a sad puppy. "Oh shit. I'm always humiliating myself with you."

Nudging her with my elbow, I ask the obvious question, "How did you remedy that problem and get your first kiss?"

Sutton pinches her lips together as if debating whether to share it with me. I nudge her again. "I'll tickle it out of you if I have to."

I get the feeling it's another embarrassing truth, but it's common for first kisses to be awkward and uncomfortable. Especially when it happens between two kids, both uncertain what to do or how to do it.

She clears her throat and lowers her eyes to her lap, evading my gaze. "It was *you*."

Her voice is so soft, and the noise of the highway so loud, I'm not sure I hear her correctly.

"Hugh? Who the hell is Hugh? I'll kick his ass."

The sound of Sutton's laughter fills the car and casts a balmy salve over my heart.

"Not Hugh. *You*." She emphasizes this remark by jabbing a finger into my biceps.

"Wait, what?"

Well, fuck all. I'm the biggest asshole in the history of all assholes.

Because for the second time in my life when it comes to Sutton, I fail to have any recollection of this kiss or when it even happened.

The delay in my response is obvious, and Sutton bites down on her bottom lip in a nervous gesture.

"You don't remember it, do you?"

I could lie. Pretend that's not the case, that I do remember kissing her silly because she's so beautiful and wonderful, and the kiss meant everything to me.

But it's not the truth.

"Button..."

She heaves a heavy sigh and then lets out a self-deprecating, half-hearted laugh.

"It's just my luck. I thought that was the case, but I wasn't one hundred percent certain. It happened the day of Mel's funeral. My mom and I had stayed behind to help Granny clean up the kitchen after everyone left, and I went upstairs to say goodbye to you when I heard you making distressing noises. I knocked on Mel's bedroom door, but you didn't answer, so I walked in to see what was going on."

My breath hitches at this memory, a dull ache throbbing in my chest that I rub my palm over in the hope it'll go away.

"As I entered, I noticed you sitting on the floor in her closet. I sat down next to you, telling you over and over again it was okay. That Melodie was in a better place then."

Vaguely I can picture it, the view from the floor of Mel's closet, the bottle of Jim Beam in my hand, my knees drawn up to my chin, and Mel's open diary laid out next to me.

The secrets it had told me about Mel's life after I went away to school. Her loneliness and pain.

And the pain she survived but remained scarred with from my stepfather's abusive hands.

It tore me open that day, and I bled out.

After that, I was just a shell of a man.

Realizing Sutton hasn't finished telling her story, I break through the silence that crept in over us and say, "I know I was drunk out of my mind. Obliterated from both my loss and the booze."

She nods, a bit of consolation and agreement. "I knew that. I smelled the whiskey and saw the half-empty bottle next to you. At that moment, I understood what you felt. What the devastating ripple effects of Mel's death would have on us. And all I wanted to do was take away your pain and provide some level of comfort."

A harsh thought races through my head, my heart pounding as fast as a speeding train. A lump of bile rises in the back of my throat, and I swallow it down like a bitter, acidic pill.

"Oh fuck, Button. Did I... I didn't come on to you, did I?"

A look of shock and repugnance crosses her face and colors her eyes a deep, forest green.

"Because that would've been so terrible if you did, Miles?"

We near a gas station and I immediately whip the car into the parking lot, finding the closest spot to park and turn off the engine.

Unbuckling my seat belt, I maneuver to face her, reaching to cup her face, turning her to face me, so there is no confusion what I mean.

"Sutton, nothing about being with you would ever be terrible. But you were seventeen—"

"Almost eighteen," she interjects with such force that I have to hide my smile for fear she might slap it right off my face.

"Whatever," I concede. "The point is, I was almost twenty-three. A grown-ass man and you were a young girl who'd never even been fucking kissed. Jesus Christ, I'm such a morally depraved asshole."

Sutton covers my hands with hers, pulling them down to her lap, absently stroking my palms.

"Miles, I didn't want this moment to be a scene. You were my first kiss. A kiss I'd dreamed about for years before. I worshipped you. I loved you from afar. I would've given you my innocence had you not been the gentleman that you are."

I groan inwardly. God, had I fucked her that day, I'd never forgive myself.

It's bad enough I failed my sister, but then to have potentially ruined her best friend and taken something so precious from her while I could barely stand up on my own, would've been unconscionable.

"I'm no gentleman, Sutton. But I'm glad I had the wherewithal not to go there with you."

She sighs, lifting her hand to place it over my heart.

"Miles Thatcher, you are a good man with a good heart. I wish you could see what I see in you. And for the record, you were the best first kiss I've ever had."

30

Sutton

"Good evening, Mr. Thatcher. It's so good to see you. Miss Iris will be pleased as punch to have you here for dinner. She's been chattering all day about her handsome, smart grandson."

I quirk an eyebrow at a blushing Miles—yes, he's blushing—as the nursing home's front desk receptionist fusses over him like he's the town celebrity.

In a way, he kind of is a hometown hero. He was a star baseball player in high school, the valedictorian of his graduating class, and then became one of the more successful former townies. And let's face it, he's super easy on the eyes and has been charming women, young and old, for years since he was just a punk kid.

As if finally realizing that Miles isn't alone, she turns to me with a smiling expression. "Well, it looks like Iris will be getting an extra guest tonight. And who might you be, my dear?"

"Hi there. My name is Sutton. Sutton Fuller."

The woman's eyes blow wide. "*My, my, my*. Little Sutton Fuller. I remember you when you were just yay high to a grasshopper." She demonstrates this by lowering her flattened palm to below her waist.

"Your mama and I used to work the church clothing drives together. I haven't seen her in ages. How is she doing, honey?"

I smile broadly, my head swiveling to look between her and Miles, who stands facing me with an amused twinkle in his eye.

"Oh, she and my dad are doing great. She's still teaching third grade at Mystic View Elementary, and pretty sure she's driving my dad crazy as usual." I chuckle. My parents have been married almost thirty years, and since I've moved out, they seem to bicker over everything. "But they're doing well."

"Well, you tell her I said to say hello." She hands me a visitor badge with my name penned neatly on the front. It has an adhesive backing which I adhere to my chest and discard the film in the wastebasket below the window.

"Thanks, Mary Jane," Miles says, accepting his and doing the same. "Do you want me to sneak you some butterscotch pudding if it's on the menu tonight?"

Miles whispers to me conspiratorially, "Don't let her sweet looks fool you. Mary Jane here has turned me into a hardened criminal and accomplice due to her butterscotch pudding addiction. And she makes me steal extra pudding cups anytime I come for dinner."

She laughs boisterously, waving a hand in the air. "Pish.

That's so untrue. You just like spoiling an old woman for sport."

I nod in agreement at her statement, raising my eyebrows in solidarity. "Isn't that the truth. He's such a flirt and charmer when he's not being broody."

Mary Jane laughs again as Miles gives us a teasing look of innocence. "I can't believe I'm being picked on when all I've been is nice to both of you." He points between us, eyebrows narrowed judgmentally.

He playfully walks off, flipping his hand in the air behind him, pretending he's all butthurt.

I roll my eyes and lean into the window. "Men. So sensitive to the truth."

"Amen, sister."

I wave goodbye to Mary Jane and rush to catch up to Miles, who has just rounded the corner of a long corridor leading into a cafeteria where the smell of Clorox disinfectant and turkey meat fills the air.

"She's a sweetheart," I comment, threading my fingers through Miles's hand. "And you really do know how to charm women. Always have."

He bestows one of those charming smiles on me, and like the giddy schoolgirl I am, I bask in its glow.

This is the Miles I remember from my childhood. The boy who could smile and use his cunning wit and boyishly good looks to get away with anything. The boy everyone loved and adored and the one the girls flocked to, hoping to be plucked from the crowd and singled out for his attention.

Miles lifts his shoulder. "What can I say? It's one of my many talents."

I snort as we enter a crowded cafeteria filled with fifteen or so circular tables, each table surrounded by elderly residents and their aides. It's not a particularly full room, but for the number of people in it, there isn't much noise.

We stop just inside the door as Miles scans the area in search of his grandmother.

"There she is." Miles lifts his chin toward a table in the back corner.

I take a step forward only to be stopped abruptly by the tug of his hand. I whip my head around to see him with apprehension sketched across his furrowed brows.

He clears his throat, voice quiet and hesitant. Completely unlike the guy who was just joking a moment ago.

"Um, I failed to mention something." He pauses, inhaling a deep breath before breathing out. I give his hand a reassuring squeeze.

"It's fine, Miles. I understand."

His gaze falls to the floor. "Granny has good days and bad. Sometimes she's the way she's always been, but sometimes, and most often, she lapses into a woman who's not all there."

"Dementia?"

His face turns to stone, eyes like dark granite in their fury over his grandmother's condition.

"Yeah. It started two years ago and has progressively gotten worse. In fact, last Saturday, before the volunteer event, I had to make an emergency trip up here because she fell and reinjured her hip. When I asked her what happened, she had no recollection of why she was in a wheelchair to begin with. I'm just warning you that. . . well, she may not know who you are."

Compressing my lips together, I give him a tight nod, hoping he knows he's not alone, and I'm here for him.

The minute we hit Iris's table, her eyes light up with the joy only a grandmother can feel when seeing a loved one.

"Miles! You're here. I've missed you."

And then she sees me, and something in her eyes flickers and stutters, a memory escaping the recesses of her mind and reemerging in a new, indiscernible appearance.

Iris's voice weakens and comes out almost as a whispered sob.

"Meli? Is that you?"

31

M*iles*

My feet falter, and it feels like my gut has been hit with a battering ram.

And by the look across Sutton's face, she's experiencing the same level of torment.

When I began talking to Granny's doctors, they indicated that lucidity is a fragile thing with dementia patients, and their brains just don't function to filter out reality, the past or the present. There is confusion, mix-ups, anger and agitation, and sometimes just pure radiant joy.

Seeing the approval and love that generates from Granny's appearance right now, in her belief that Sutton is her granddaughter, is too much to squash by telling her otherwise.

Sutton's head turns to stare at me with the unspoken question of "*What do I do*?"

I take the problem off her hands and respond to Granny, bending down to kiss her weathered and wrinkly cheek. "Hi, Granny. Look who I brought with me tonight for dinner."

Tears gather in the corner of her eyes, and I can barely stand here in this lie. But what else am I supposed to do? Tell her she's wrong, that Sutton isn't her granddaughter because Mel's dead?

It would be a recipe for disaster. Granny wouldn't be able to comprehend or disassociate this present reality with what she believes to be true in her mind. And no matter what I would say to correct her assumptions, it would only create a further disconnect and then an outburst of frustration.

Not happening.

I offer a chair next to Granny's wheelchair for Sutton to sit down, and I take the next seat over. There's another woman on the opposite side of the table, but she's hunched over her plate mumbling something incoherently.

God bless her.

"Melodie, my sweet, beautiful girl. Where have you been? I haven't seen you in ages."

Sutton blinks, and I can see the thoughts forming in her head, as they roll around and gather steam before exiting her mouth in a lie I've basically demanded her to perform.

Sutton places a hand over Granny's and leans in to kiss her forehead. The gesture has a lump forming in my throat.

"Hi, Granny. I'm so sorry I haven't been here in a while. You know, I've just been so busy going to school and working in the city."

Sutton flicks a hopeful glance at me, looking for further direction, and I blink, gesturing with a nod for her to keep going.

I feel like a prick for not warning Sutton what we might

encounter today. It's just such a crapshoot from day to day, and impossible to predict what version of my grandmother I'll find when I show up.

Granny smiles proudly. "Oh, I'm so proud of you. Are you still swimming? You were always so fast in the water. I called you my little fish, do you remember?"

Sutton's voice is thick with emotion that makes something inside me crack open. Fuck me, but this girl—*this woman*—is the best thing that's ever happened in my life.

"I still swim, Granny. And Miles still seems to beat me."

Granny's attention returns back to me, and I try to fake my enthusiasm, stuffing the pain ripping me to shreds back inside my chest like a life-size Build-a-Bear experiment.

"Our Miles is hard to beat, that's for sure. He was born to be a winner. He came early, you know, letting only one shrill cry out into the world. A tiny war-cry telling everyone know he was going to take the world by storm."

I stifle the eye roll that wants to let loose, but how can I not be flattered to hear the adoring words from my own grandmother.

Looking at how little my grandmother has eaten, I encourage her to continue and invite Sutton with me to the cafeteria-style conveyor line.

"We'll be right back, Granny. Don't run off anywhere, okay?"

The words couldn't ring truer. I'm not worried about her leaving physically, but who knows if the woman here with us will be the same one five minutes from now.

As I usher Sutton to the buffet, I can't help but apologize for putting her in this compromising position.

"I'm sorry if this is awkward, Button."

Sutton grabs a tray, passing it to me and picks up another one before sliding it over the metal counter. "Miles, you have nothing to apologize for. It just makes me sad to know you've been dealing with this all on your own. How long has she been here?"

I reach for a plate of spaghetti, the sauce runny and smelling heavy on the garlic, along with a prepared bowl of salad, setting them on my tray as I follow closely behind Sutton.

"A few months now. She's only been noticeably declining over the past six months. Until then, she was sharp as a tack, only forgetting basic things, which is why I let her remain living alone in the house. But one day I got a call from the fire department while I was on a business trip in Dallas. She'd put oil in a pan to cook something and then forgot about it, leaving the stovetop burner on. Thank God the smoke detector went off and the alarm company called nine-one-one. When they found her, she was huddled in the corner of her bedroom, panicked and unresponsive."

Sutton's eyes hold sympathetic concern, her hand gripping my forearm with kind solidarity.

"Miles, that must've been awful, especially being so far away and unable to race home."

We get to the end of the counter, and I pull my wallet out, handing the woman a fifty. The meals are included in my grandmother's plan, but any guests are required to pay.

"Keep the change," I offer as we head back to the table where my grandmother is now talking to an aide.

The man straightens as we walk up and place our trays down on the table.

"Is everything okay?" I ask him, his braided hair pulled up in a thick ponytail behind his head.

"Ah, yes. I was just checking in on my gal, Iris. She seemed a bit disoriented."

Sutton and I lock eyes, both alarmed at the sudden change in her demeanor.

"Granny, are you okay?"

My grandmother stares down at her plate of half-eaten food, mumbling something on repeat. I'm not sure what flipped the switch since we were only gone a few minutes, but when I place my palm gently on her shoulder, she stiffens.

And then screams.

Loudly and unceasing.

Sutton's hand flies to her mouth, and I jerk back in alarm. Josh, the nurse's aide, looks at us and shrugs.

"It's okay. This happens. I'll take her back to her room and get her settled. Maybe give her fifteen minutes to regroup."

As he wheels her away from the table, her shrieks continuing in an on-and-off cycle, I throw myself down in the seat and hang my head in my hands, massaging my temples to thwart the tension headache already building at the base of my skull.

"Goddamn it. I can't do this anymore."

Somewhere from outside my misery, I hear Sutton's calming voice. "Shh. . . it's okay, Miles. You'll get through this. I'm here for you."

When I lift my head and find Sutton on her knees in front of me, I know she's both wrong and right.

She is here for me and for that I'm grateful.

But I honestly don't know how I'm going to make it through this tortured and prolonged deterioration of my grandmother. For every step forward, she takes four steps further away from me and from reality.

And reality bites like a motherfucker.

32

Sutton

It's just after eight p.m. when we decide to return to Miles's childhood home for the night, the house his grandmother left behind when she moved into the nursing facility. We'd stopped by my parents' house for a brief chat, but after the confrontation with his Granny, Miles was visibly worn out, so we didn't stay long.

My mother gave me a curious lift of her brow before we left her house but didn't say a word when I mentioned staying the night with Miles. Not that she'd say anything anyway, since I'm a twenty-five-year-old adult who no longer lives under their roof or by their rules.

Our three-block walk between the two homes is relatively quiet, as we hold hands and maneuver the streets that I've known by heart since I was a kid.

"Miles," I whisper, my voice sounding abnormally loud

in the quiet silence of the mid-summer evening. "I'm not going to pry or push, but have you considered talking to a therapist?"

I'd been contemplating saying something to him since I found him in the hallway weeks ago, knowing how far gone he was over all that he's lost over the years. And the burden also includes the decline of his grandmother's health and mental fitness. It's just too much for any one person to bear alone.

Miles snaps his eyes down to me. "For what?"

Whether he's pretending or is just resistant to the idea, I don't know. But I'm not going to sidestep this important suggestion.

"A grief counselor. For the feelings and emotions you've obviously shut down all these years, that are likely resurfacing with your granny's situation."

He makes a scoffing noise. "I'm good. Thanks."

He uses a key and unlocks the door into the small, three-bedroom bungalow-style home his grandmother no longer occupies. As we step across the threshold, I can still smell the spices that used to waft through the kitchen and hear traces of the arguments between brother and sister that always seemed to occur. He may have been a protective older brother to Melodie, but that doesn't mean he didn't love to antagonize the hell out of his little sister.

I'm about to say more about the need for counseling when Miles shuts and locks the door and, without a word, reaches for my wrist and pulls me into the living room.

"All the help I need is right here in this room with me tonight."

I lick my lips as his descend on mine, nipping hard and sampling me like I'm his dessert he passed on earlier.

Whimpering at the slight sting of his kiss, my breath hitches when he speaks against my lips.

"I need your mouth on my cock again, Sutton. I want to give these beautiful full lips all the attention they deserve and watch them wrap around my cock and see it disappear in your mouth."

Mmm, yes, I want that too.

I drop my hand between us to the front of his jeans, grasping his erection that bulges underneath. Stroking up and down with enough pressure to ensure it's felt all the way down to his toes, I get a flutter of satisfaction as he grunts with pleasure.

"On your knees, Button."

The command elicits an unsuppressed shiver that runs up my spine. Before I drop to the floor, Miles cups my face and kisses me with endearing tenderness. So contradictory from his rough, sexy commands. My breasts rise and fall with heaviness, nipples distending with the need to be plucked and teased.

Falling to my knees, I reach for his belt, unbuckling and then unzipping as I take his cock out, the sight of it making my mouth water with anticipation. Miles shimmies out of his jeans, pushing them down to the floor and out of the way. He then reaches down and lifts my shirt over my head and unclasps my bra.

"I want to feel these jiggle in my touch every time you swallow me down," he says while cupping my breasts before moving one hand to guide my head toward his swollen cock.

My thighs clench at his dirty words and devious deeds, and there is no one else I'd want to tell me these naughty fantasies.

My fingers lace around the base of his shaft, hard and

satiny soft all at once, and lick the top of the crown. I swirl my tongue around the rim, flicking the sensitive slit and then wrap my lips around him firmly. With each action, each deliberate move, I extract a groan from Miles's throat and chest, and there is no better sound in the world to my ears.

His thrusts soon become rough, breaths ragged, as I continue to suck and lick and swallow him down, moaning around his throbbing girth. It doesn't take long before his hips jerk unevenly, his panting loud, and his fingers steel their grip in my hair, controlling the pace of my moves.

"I'm close, Button. So fucking close. I want to see you swallow me down, baby. Every fucking drop."

The words are music to my ears, flooding my panties with arousal so hot, I can't stop myself from touching myself.

When I slip my hand down my shorts, my fingers easily glide over my wet sex. I moan, the vibration striking a chord and turning Miles into a beast.

Miles palms my breast roughly, plumping and squeezing, my nipple pebbling stiffly and shooting zings of pleasure to my clit. My climax hits me hard, abruptly, and violently as I cry out. At the same time, Miles's grip tightens in my hair, and his body stills. His cock begins pulsing as a stream of hot liquid hits the back of my throat, coating my tongue, sliding down my throat as I swallow all of him just like he asked.

I blink up at him from below, my mouth still full of him to find his gaze has gone soft with post-orgasm afterglow. He slowly disengages, pulling his semi-hard dick from my mouth, and uses a thumb to wipe away the remnants of him from across my lip.

I take his offered hand and stand to my feet as he angles his head into my neck and nibbles my skin. He continues biting his way up to my earlobe, where he tugs it between his teeth.

"Did I see you finger fucking yourself to orgasm?" he asks, just as easily as he could have asked me if the sky is blue.

I nod sheepishly. "Yes."

"Give me that hand."

Chewing on my lip, I deliberate for a second and then lift the hand I used to finger myself. My fingers are coated with my essence, and the menacing stare from Miles makes me think I've done something wrong. He snags my wrist without warning, the action so sharp I snap my head back.

And then I watch with parted lips as he sucks my fingers into his mouth, the tip of his tongue flicking over my fingertips, and then pulls them back out.

The corners of my lips curve up into a sideways grin, and I cheekily ask, "Miles? What are your thoughts on fucking me in your childhood bed?"

A boom of laughter erupts from his chest. "I'd have to say I have plenty of thoughts on that. Let me demonstrate."

33

Miles

THE MORNING SUN streams in through the old, plaid curtains of my childhood bedroom, casting enough light to color the room in warm, orangish-yellow hues. And to paint a sleeping Sutton in an angelic glow.

But I know the truth now about Sutton. She is far from an angel after all the dirty fucking we did last night.

Her hair cascades over the pillow like an autumn leaf falling to the ground. She sleeps curled in a tight cocoon, her hands drawn up under her chin in a prayer position.

And dear God, did I hear her screaming the lord's name over and over again last night in feverish prayer as we came together several times in unlawful carnal knowledge.

Which has me horny-as-fuck right now just thinking about it.

I thought it would be weird to sleep with her in my

childhood bedroom. In a house where we grew up, where every room holds a memory of a young Sutton and my sister. Where I would chase them around like a lunatic, pretending to be a monster. Or play *Go Fish* or board games, or I'd tell them ghost stories on Halloween after we returned from trick-or-treating and rummaged through our loot.

But none of those memories warranted a moment's consideration as I slid into her each time, her willingness to accept me for who I am and who I've been is the only thing that brings me any measure of comfort these days.

As if she knows I'm thinking about her, Sutton rolls over to her back to find me blatantly ogling her naked form.

"What are you staring at?" Her morning voice is raspy and throaty, not dissimilar to the way her voice rasped last night.

I place a kiss on her bare shoulder and trail my finger over her collarbone, descending a path between her cleavage, discarding the sheet as I go.

"This has to be the best sleepover I've ever had in this house."

Sutton blushes, giggling from under her arm that covers her face. "But I have morning breath and messy hair and no make-up."

"None of which I care about because you are beautiful any time of day." I remove her arm from her face and brush the strands of hair out of her eyes. "I'm just sorry it took me so goddamn long to figure that out, Button."

She rolls to the side to face me, my palm dropping to her shoulder as I run my knuckles over the smooth velvety skin I've been itching to touch since I woke earlier this morning.

I've actually been awake for an hour now. After using the bathroom, letting Blackie outside and feeding him, and putting on a pot of coffee, I returned to watch a sleeping

Sutton. I tried to conjure up all the memories I could of her and Mel back in the day, and if at any point, I saw her as anything more than my sister's friend.

Perhaps had there not been such a noticeable age gap as kids, it might have been different. But by the time I left for college, she and Mel were still in middle school, jailbait for an eighteen-year-old guy. And it never dawned on me to think twice about Button.

The fact that I have no recollection of the kiss we shared the day of Mel's funeral is just a travesty. By that time, Sutton was a senior in high school and had matured enough not to be seen as a little girl or kid. I'm sure she was just as striking then as she is now. She has a natural beauty and sensual sweetness that radiates outwardly to the world.

All I remember of that day is that I was mired in grief and completely inconsolable. Filled with so much anger and rage over losing my baby sister that I was blind to anything or anyone around me. Even the beautiful, starry-eyed girl who was eager to share in my grief and be a shoulder to cry on.

Sutton smiles up through her long lashes, and I bend down to kiss the top of her forehead.

"We can't change the past, Miles. But I'm really liking the direction the future is taking now."

A phone buzzing in the distance pulls us out of our bubble, and I pat around the bed to see if I can find it. Sutton rolls to the side, grabbing her phone, scrolling through some texts as they appear on her display, and her eyes grow wide with panicked shock.

"Oh my God," she says, throwing off the sheet and jumping out of bed, searching the vicinity for her clothes. "I've got to go home, Miles. It's my boss, my friend Lucy. It's her son. They're at Children's Hospital. He has to go in for emergency surgery. I. . . I. . ."

I roll out of bed, throwing on some shorts and a T-shirt that I found in the dresser bureau as I go in search of the lost articles of clothing deposited last night somewhere on the floor.

When I return to the bedroom, tears flow down Sutton's sad face, and she's trembling out of shock.

"Hey, Button. You're okay." I sit down on the bed next to her, cradling her in my open arms. "We'll go back, but there's nothing you can do in the meantime except let her know you're coming, and you're praying for her. Can you do that? Or do you want me to text her?"

She hands me the phone with quaking hands and runs to the bathroom and slams the door behind her, where I hear her sobbing in inconsolable grief.

Ah, shit. My poor Button.

And I understand what it's like to be unable to take away someone else's pain and agony from them.

I type out a brief text to Lucy on her phone and head toward the hallway, waiting for Sutton to wash up.

"Are you okay now?" I ask her through the bathroom door.

Her weak response tells me she's lying. "Yeah, I'll be fine. Just give me a little bit."

"Of course. I'll be right here when you're ready to go."

I begin pacing the hallway and end up on the far end where Mel's old room had been. The door is shut, probably not been opened for over a year. I'm not sure how often Granny had gone in there. For me, there's still far too many memories and ghosts living in this room. But seeing as I have nothing but time to wait, I open the door and step in.

It's been seven years since I've stepped foot into this room. How strange is that?

There are posters of bands I've never heard of on the wall, a desk in the corner with framed pictures and books, knick-knacks, and swimming trophies. I see three frames on the wall shelf, along with a wooden box decorated with painted flowers in yellow and pink.

I stare at one of the framed pictures of Mel and me on my high school graduation day. I'm a foot and a half taller than her, so I'm bent over her like a tree, casting a shadow over her small form, my bright blue tassel from my cap dangling in her face. Her smile is big and bright. And she looked so happy.

What went wrong, Mel? Why didn't I see it?

Another picture grabs my attention. This one is Mel and a younger Sutton. They're both in swimsuits, their gangly teen arms flung around each other's shoulders in proud celebration, with medals hanging from their necks. It must've been from one of their middle school swim meets where they'd finished in first and second place. Their smiles tell it all.

Sutton's smile hasn't changed in the least, even though her appearance is so vastly different from her pre-pubescent days. At that age, she was a tall, skinny girl with toothpicks for legs. Short cropped hair that never seemed to lay flat and teeth that bucked out in the front with a bit of a gap in the middle. There's hardly any resemblance to the woman she is now.

"I remember that day like it was yesterday."

Sutton's voice startles me as she steps into my peripheral view, reaching for the photo and picking it up in her grasp. Her smile is wan, but filled with a tender sadness, as she replaces it on the shelf.

"She was such a natural swimmer. Competitive to a fault, but she was always striving to achieve perfection. God, Miles. She would've gone so far in whatever career or field she chose. I just wish. . ."

I close my arms around her and hold her, clinging to our connection and the spirit of Mel.

"I know, Button. I know. I wish, too."

34

S*utton*

MILES DROPPED Blackie and me off at the apartment so I could shower and change before rushing back over to the store. Lucy indicated no visitors were allowed just yet for Antonio at the hospital, but I was getting regular updates from her via text as she learned more from the doctor on the status of his condition.

She said they'd diagnosed him with pediatric Crohn's disease, an inflammatory bowel disease that may require surgery to remove an inflamed part of his intestine. My heart sank as I read her texts.

Lucy: Dr says they won't know the extent of the damage until they have a CT scan and ultrasound. Then they might have to perform surgery.

Lucy: My baby boy might have to have a portion of his colon removed.

Lucy: I am not okay.

I racked my brain trying to think of something —*anything*—that I could do to alleviate her pain and worry, but it's impossible to do. She has her family and husband, Juan, by her side, and all I can do is let her know I'll take care of things at the store, so she doesn't have to worry.

Me: I'm so sorry, Lucy. Please don't worry about the shop, I'll take care of things for you. Just stay strong and know I'll be here if you need me. Praying for you and Antonio. Xoxo

The words rang true, but hollow, as I could only console in her time of need. No mother should have to go through that with their children, and it broke my heart for this woman, who through insurmountable odds, raised three children and built a business that flourished through her tireless pursuit of perfection.

The weight of despair weighs heavily on my mind and heart as I finally get to the store to relieve the other part-time employee, Camilla, who is assisting with a customer at the moment.

Traipsing into the back storeroom, I lock my purse away in the small footlocker Lucy has for each of us and pin my nametag on my shirt. I check the clipboard hanging on the wall to see there's a delivery scheduled for today, which means I'll be handling inventory late into the evening tonight.

Which is just as well, it'll help me keep my mind off of everything going on—with both Lucy and Miles.

What a crazy, wild, and emotional trip it was back to Mystic. While Miles didn't become overly defensive when I mentioned grief counseling to him, he didn't exactly seem thrilled by the prospect, either.

As a student of psychology, it seems clearly obvious to

me that Miles has suppressed his grief over the years, and it's eating away at him, just as Antonio's gut disease is doing to him. The two things may be unlike in how they manifest in a person, but each equally, and without compassion, will tear at the fabric of their internal systems and destroy them if not handled properly.

For Antonio, it may mean surgery and a lifetime of medications and treatments.

For Miles, it could be managed by seeing a therapist and unloading all that grief he's been holding onto for years.

The remainder of the day passes by relatively quickly, the shop being busy on a weekend day. Miles texted me once, earlier on in the day, and I responded with a quick, "talk later" reply because we'd been slammed.

When I did finally get a chance to text him a real reply, I mentioned I'd be working late after the shop closed to handle the inventory and restocking.

Miles: Can I bring you something to eat?

Me: You are so sweet. You don't have to, but I'd love it.

Miles: Oh, you meant food. My bad. I had something else in mind for you to eat.

My shoulders shake from my laughter as I read his naughty text, as another one comes in right after.

Miles: Just kidding. Sort of. I'll be by in thirty minutes with Chinese. That good?

Me: Both sound delicious.

I insert a smiley face and an eggplant emoji for good measure because Miles brings out both the naughty girl in me and the one that is just ecstatic to have him back in my life in this manner.

It's crazy to think how time can change people. Seven years ago, as Miles pointed out, I didn't possess the maturity or meet the age requirement to be with a twenty-three-year-old man. It would've been wrong, regardless of the circumstances.

But now that I'm an adult, things are different. The relationship can be different. And we can start something that might lead into something longer-term.

It dawns on me that Graham and Soraya will be returning home soon. I check the calendar on the wall, and sure enough, they'll be returning on Wednesday of this week. I need to confirm with Ben that I can move in again until I can find a new place, either with roommates or an inexpensive apartment of my own.

A pang in my heart ripples and quakes, and I swallow down my sadness. It'll be weird not seeing Miles every day, whether by chance or planned meet-up. I've become used to having him knock on my door in the mornings to head downstairs for a swim or workout. Or a walk in the park with him and Blackie in the late evenings, before climbing into one of our beds and fooling around before falling asleep in each other's arms.

Miles is everything I'd ever thought he would be as a boyfriend, and the guy I'd always dreamed of being with.

Yet I feel there is a loose strand of yarn threatening to unravel the woven fabric of this thing building between us. Miles has admitted to not dating or having a single lasting relationship since he was in high school. What does that mean for me? For us?

Perhaps I'm romanticizing our affair between us due to my longstanding feelings for Miles. The fascination over him, the crush I've harbored for years with all the wanting and yearning to be with him.

To be someone to Miles other than a fling or a fuck buddy.

To be someone special in his eyes.

35

Miles

As I wait for the Chinese takeout, sitting in a God-awful, orange plastic chair, I type out a quick text to Graham.

Me: Hey, buddy. Just checking in again. Hope you're enjoying your last few days of rest and relaxation.

I get an immediate reply.

Graham: Consensus is "*We're never coming home.*" So, I'll start the paperwork to sell you the business.

My loud snorting chuckle garners curious glances from the other three patrons hanging out in the small restaurant waiting for their orders. A sidelong look from an elderly woman makes me want to laugh louder, but I tamp down the need to annoy her and clamp my lips together and return the text.

Me: Gladly. Any day. And let's face it, I'm the far better choice. You're a lazy ass.

An image appears on my phone, and this time I can't help my laughter. It's Graham, lying on a lounge chair, hat pulled down to shade his eyes, a beer bottle in his clasped hand, and his bare chest sunburned like a cooked lobster.

Me: Jesus, dude. Ever hear of SPF?

Graham: (Flipping the bird emoji)

Graham: That was from last week. I'm back to a nice tan again. But I have to say, not terribly excited about returning. How's my dog-sitter doing? You checked in on her lately?

I make a coughing sound, clearing the reluctance that sits in my throat to mention anything. But it's Graham, and he won't give a shit, especially when he finds out the circumstances involving Sutton's and my relationship.

My fingers tap across my phone.

Me: Funny you should mention...

Graham: I knew it! You tapped that, didn't you? Mofo. Just couldn't resist the temptation, could you?

Me: It's a weird story. I finally learned why she seemed so familiar to me. She was Melodie's best friend.

Because I've known Graham since grad school, he is very aware of what happened to my family and Mel's death. In fact, had it not been for Graham, I'm not sure I could've gotten back on track after returning to school. As it was, it took me months to return to some semblance of normal and get my study habits and grades back to where they were prior to Mel's funeral.

Graham: You were that oblivious not to recognize her? You are a self-absorbed asshat, you know that, right?

Miles: You don't know the half of it. But yeah, she's not the same girl I once knew.

Three dots appear and then disappear as if he's

consulting with his *Ask Ida* expert slash wife to help him dictate his note.

Finally, his response pops up, and it's a bit unnerving because it hits too close to home.

Graham: Be careful there. She's young and you're not. Just be clear of your expectations so you don't hurt her.

Graham: This is Soraya, btw. Sorry, I couldn't resist.

I knew it! I figured any relationship advice or comments would automatically be pawned off on his wife.

Me: Appreciate the advice, *Ida*. Safe travels home. See you all soon.

It will be nice to have them back in town. While I see Graham every day in the office, and some nights during impromptu happy hours, I don't often get a chance to hang with Soraya. Being the third wheel around those two lovebirds is enough to drive a guy nuts. But they are a great couple and one that I hope I can spend more time with if things continue with Sutton.

While I'm still not interested in a relationship, I've rather enjoyed dating and getting to know Sutton as an adult these past weeks. I can see things progressing further, as long as she understands I'm not boyfriend material or a man that's going to offer her marriage.

The husband and father role model I had in my life taught me one big lesson: don't get married or have children. And don't, under any circumstances, take on the role of stepfather.

None of that is anywhere on my Top 100 things to do in the next ten years.

Or maybe ever.

36

Sutton

"Oh my God, this is so delicious." The moan I give after the first bite of my orange chicken would make even the highest-rated porn star blush.

And it garners a sexy eyebrow quirk from my dinner date.

Miles and I sit cross-legged on the floor in the breakroom, a term I use loosely since it doubles as the stock room, with a small mini fridge, a microwave on a stand, and a coffee maker on a makeshift platform. We sit, slurping up noodles, fried rice, and the most melt-in-your-mouth orange chicken I've ever tasted.

It could also be out of this world for the sheer fact that I haven't eaten since breakfast and that I'm sharing it with Miles.

He wipes a napkin over his lips and the corners of his mouth lift in a sly grin. "You keep moaning like that, and I'm going throw you over that pile of boxes over there and have my way with you."

"Mmm, that sounds good too. But let me finish this first."

Miles shakes his head and laughs, reaching over and plucking a piece of chicken from my plate with his chopsticks. I quickly engage my own, wielding them like a sword, to prevent him from stealing any more. He laughs and raises his hands in surrender.

"Aggressive, much?"

I lift my shoulders and shove some greasy noodles in my mouth, slurping the slippery goodness through my lips and tilting my head in victory over not spilling a bit. My chopsticks skills are not up to par, at least not like they are for Miles.

"How are you so good with these?" I ask, waving around the wooden chopsticks between us.

Miles scoops up some rice, adding some vegetables, and takes a giant bite, as I watch his strong jaw work as he chews.

He follows his bite with a sip of water from the bottle, my eyes glued to the way his Adam's apple bobs and moves as he swallows it down. How can eating be such a turn-on? It feels like a flip has been switched in me, and I've become ravenous for sex.

When I'm not with Miles, I'm thinking about what we've done together in bed, or what he will be doing to me. And when he's present, it's all I can do to restrain myself from tearing off my clothes and begging him to do wicked things to me.

His knowing grin, and the way his tongue rolls over his

bottom lip, tells me he has a pretty good inkling what I'm thinking about.

"Right after grad school, and before I went to work for Graham, I took a month and traveled to Asia. The culture always intrigued me, and I had a good friend at Yale, Ming Su, that grew up in China, and her family still lived there. They were gracious enough to let me stay with them for a few weeks, and it was fascinating and beautiful. I learned a lot from their culture, and I think it helped. . ."

I glance up from my takeout container to find Miles staring off over my shoulder, lost in thought.

"It helped to get away from your grief for a while?"

His eyes flick back to mine, lips compressed tightly as he nods. "Yeah, that. And it kept the memories at bay and helped me find my will to live again. I took up some Tai Chi practices and learned some of the Buddhist monks' philosophies. It was pretty powerful stuff."

"That sounds cool. Do you still practice?"

His head drops, shaking it as he spears another vegetable piece. "Nah, I don't. I really should, though."

"When I lived with my friend, Christiana, we, along with our friend, Taylor, would attend yoga classes twice a week. More if we had time. I think we pile on so much in our heads from everyday life that we become polluted with negative energy and emotional baggage, and it manifests as toxins in our body. We need those outlets to detox our bodies to free ourselves from it all, you know?"

"I agree," he nods, setting his food aside and moving to his hands and knees to crawl to where I sit. "You know what other physical activity works great for reducing stress?"

I giggle when he leans in and bites my neck, licking a swath of skin underneath my ear.

Without even a look, he removes the container and utensils from my hands, setting them aside, and covers me with his body, as he lies me down on the floor.

Staring up into his gorgeous eyes, I quirk a smile. "No, but I bet you're about to educate me on that option."

With one hand propping him up over me, he slips his other hand between us, lifting the material of my skirt, brushing his knuckles over my sensitive thighs.

A shiver runs down my spine, goosebumps breaking out over my skin, as his mouth latches to my neck, sucking a path down my chest and his fingers simultaneously work their magic over my panties.

"Remove your shirt and bra," he commands in a growl. "I need to feel you."

I do as he asks, quickly unbuttoning, unclasping, and divesting myself of the layers of clothing between us, while his fingers tease over my clit through the silk of my panties.

With my breasts now bare, Miles drops his head to cover my nipple with his mouth, pulling it between his teeth and then laving over it with his wet tongue. I writhe underneath him from the pleasure he bestows. My nipples so hard and sensitive, the sensations shooting straight to my core, my inner walls clenching in unison crying out to be filled by him. By his cock.

"Miles," I murmur. "I want you inside me."

He edges underneath my panties, his finger skimming over the swollen nub, my hips darting off the floor, and without preamble, eases two fingers inside.

I groan loudly from the intrusion, his fingers stretching me, filling me, curling and hitting that perfect spot that has me trembling with need. Need for more.

"You're a greedy little girl, aren't you, Button?"

"Mmm. Yes. Please."

While none of my pleas make any sense, they're on a constant loop as he continues to overwhelm me with pleasure, his filthy words and spoken fantasies driving me closer and closer to my release.

"I want you on top and riding me, your tits jiggling in my face."

"I want to fuck you bare. Come inside your sweet pussy."

And oh, my word, every image curated by his filthy mouth takes me to places I've never been before with anyone else.

His thumb rubs over my clit, his mouth sucking my tight pebbled nipple in his mouth, as I hoarsely cry out my release.

"Miles. . . oh God. . . Miles." My head thrashes back and forth, my body tightens. I come with such intensity it feels like I've been shot into outer space from the force in which I orgasm.

No sooner do I return to Earth from that high, when Miles slips off his jeans, throws my skirt up over my belly, yanks aside my panties, and slams his cock inside me hard.

His girth stretches me wide, my pussy clenching as I claw my fingers down his back, slipping underneath the material of his T-shirt, scoring down the strained muscles of his backside, digging and scraping to get him closer.

I need all of him. Anything less just won't do.

During one of our rounds back home this weekend, when Miles had run out of condoms in the middle of the night, we'd talked about birth control and all the exceedingly unsexy, yet important discussion topics of protected sex. Since I am on oral birth control, and we both are clear, we've been bare the last few times. Neither of us has ever been this way with anyone else, and it thrilled me to know I was his first like this.

"Oh fuck, baby. You feel so good. So wet. So hot. So perfect."

I bloom, like a sunflower under the sun's rays, from his compliment. Miles thinks I'm perfect. I'm perfect for him.

I eagerly trail my hands down his backside, wrapping my legs around him, heels digging into the curve of his ass. Beads of sweat break out over his forehead, his powerful thighs working to piston his hips, his muscular arms giving him leverage as he moves over me.

His hand reaches under the crook of my knee to draw it up toward my shoulder. A moan slips free from the new depth it provides, each thrust hitting something deeper inside me. Breaking me and ripping me to shreds in the most delicious way possible.

He rocks over me, his heart hammering loudly, and with a guttural groan, he throws his head back and surrenders to his release with a shuddering breath and a shout.

The aftershock has my inner walls clenching, as I feel his cock pulsing his hot release inside me. The sick thrill of knowing that I'm dripping with him has a fresh orgasm building low in my belly.

I latch on to his ass cheeks, locking him against me, jutting my hips upward to continue the friction.

"I'm going to come again."

I barely get the words out, as Miles continues to work me over, sucking my tongue into his mouth and grinding his hips in a circular motion when another orgasm tears through me.

This time, I'm coming so long and hard that my ears ring from the intensity of the explosions detonating deep within my walls.

And at the same time, my heart splits open, knowing that what I feel for Miles is no longer a teenage crush or sweet admiration.

No, it's turned into full-blown love.

"I love you, Miles."

37

M*iles*

It's been over three days since I've seen Sutton.

Part of that distance is that I've been buried up to my eyeballs in preparation for Graham's return to the office today. He texted me late Monday night indicating he'd be in the office around ten this morning, so I've spent the last few days scrubbing the reports and data he's requested, making them shine and sparkle so when he returns he knows he left his business in good hands.

After our take-out date and her late night of inventory at the shop, Sutton has spent her days and nights prepping for the Morgan's return home, as well as keeping a vigilant bedside support for her friend's son, who went through major surgery.

Although we've been texting and talking several times a

day, I've used my work and long hours as an excuse to pull back.

My entire world flipped on its axis the other night the minute Sutton muttered those words. If there are land-speed records for high-tailing it out of a woman's arms after they've just said *I love you*, I think I broke them.

Fuck me, I'm such a coward.

The moment she said them, it was obvious she was freaked out by the panicked look that flew across her face, and the way she backpedaled trying to erase the words that could never be taken back.

She chalked it up to post-coital bliss, which I gave her a pass on because it was some pretty fucking amazing sex. I was still seeing white stars behind my eyelids by the time I got home and into bed.

While I'm still not interested in a full-flown relationship, there are no doubts in my mind that I care deeply for Sutton. She's been a bright spot in my life this past month once I realized how attracted I was to her. And I'll admit, it's more than a physical attraction. It's more than I've ever felt for another woman.

But is it love? I don't know because that's not something I can commit to feeling. My heart stopped feeling that particular emotion the day I buried my sister. It broke and shattered like glass on the sidewalk, and the pieces left to be kicked and stomped on by passersby.

Am I using this unintentional time away from Sutton as a breather? As a way to run from my petrified state of mind and hide like a child does when it's seen something scary?

Fuck yeah, I am.

It's a pitiful, cowardly thing to do, but I told Sutton right from the start I wasn't the man she needs, or she deserves. Never mind the fact that the husband and father role model

I had in my life taught me one big lesson: don't get married or have children. And don't, under any circumstances, take the role of stepfather.

None of that is anywhere on my Top 100 things to do in the next ten years.

Or maybe ever.

A voice from my office doorway shakes me from my thoughts.

"I think I should go on holiday more often if this place is going to run as smoothly as it did."

I look up to see a wide smile stretched across Graham's tanned face. Sure enough, his sunburn evened out into a nice, golden tan. Motherfucker looks like a Greek god.

Pushing back from my desk, I stand and stride over to Graham, offering my hand as we clasp each other and go in for a bro-hug, slapping each other on the back.

"Welcome back, skipper. Good to have your lazy-ass back in the office."

Graham takes a seat in one of the visitor chairs and stretches his long legs out before him as I round the corner of my desk and sit back down.

Graham shakes his head. "I think this was the first vacation I've taken in"—he ticks off his fingers—"well, since just after grad school."

"It certainly seems to agree with you. You look like a fucking million bucks." I let out a humoring laugh. "Oh wait, you *are* worth over a million dollars because that's how much I made you in your absence."

We both chuckle at my joke, but then his shrewd eyes pin me with a hard-assessing stare.

"You, on the other hand, look like you could either use some sleep or a vacation of your own. What's up with this?"

Graham circles an index finger in the air toward me, highlighting the obvious bags under my eyes from exhaustion.

I flip him my middle finger. “Bro, I’ve been working my ass off here while you’ve been sipping umbrella drinks in paradise.”

He chortles and gives me disbelieving raise of his brow. “Really, is that it? All work and no play makes Miles a sad boy?”

“Whatever, man. But hey, I have those reports you wanted to see for Wales and Crawford.” I type a few keystrokes on my laptop, hoping to divert our conversation into less choppy waters.

Albeit reluctantly, Graham gives me a nod and turns his attention toward the slew of financials I’ve been working on, and we begin hashing out plans for the coming month.

Redirecting works like a charm.

Later in the day, after I’ve finished up with a client call, I check my messages to find a few texts from Sutton.

The first one is a photo of her trying on a new dress they got in at the shop. She’s draped in a see-through gauzy floral dress, ruffles at the capped shoulders, and a scoop neck in the front to show off her cleavage.

She captions it with: **Do I look like a grandma in this dress?**

I can’t help but chuckle. Sutton could never look like a grandma even in a gunny sack, which I tell her in my reply.

Her reply back is immediate.

Button: I’m over at Lucy’s tonight cooking dinner for her kids. Can I bring you some extra?

Recalling she’d mentioned that Lucy and her family live in Brooklyn, I consider the distance and the time it would take to get to my place and decline the offer.

Me: Not tonight, Button. I'm beat. I'm sure you are too after moving back to Ben's. Maybe tomorrow?

We didn't even get a chance to say goodbye this week after she'd packed up and returned to her cousin's place. Although she's been frantically looking for a place to rent before her school year begins, she hasn't been successful yet in pinning one down.

You could offer up your place.

The thought comes unbidden and out of nowhere. It's not like I hadn't considered it before now, because sleeping in the same bed every night with Sutton would be heaven. I don't think I've ever wanted to cuddle with a woman after sex, but holding my Button in my arms as we fall asleep is the most calming thing in the world.

Sutton *is* the most calming influence I've had on my life. But, she also scares me shitless.

And her response tells me that I'm making a mess of things and pushing away possibly the best woman I've ever met.

Sutton: Sure. No prob. Good night, Miles.

38

S*utton*

Dear Ida,

I made a mistake. One that might have cost me something valuable.

You see, I've been dating this guy from my past who I've reunited with by chance. At first, he didn't recognize me or remember who I was, because he hasn't seen me in years, but that problem was resolved. After reconnecting, our attraction grew, and we started dating. And that's been an amazing gift because he's a wonderful man, not at all the stuck-up big shot I originally thought he was.

But here's the problem. I opened my big fat mouth and the words, "I love you" came spilling out.

Falling in love with him was easy because I've always loved him. But it's too soon and too early in this relationship to say it.

And I think it freaked him out because he's been distant ever since.

What should I do? Just hang tight and pretend it never happened? Or reiterate that it was a mistake in a moment of passion?

I don't want to lose him. Please help.

Fool in Love

I wrote the letter and sent it via email yesterday, finding a response in my inbox right away this morning. I read it on the subway to the NYU bookstore, where I'm meeting Christiana to purchase our textbooks for the semester. The words in *Ask Ida's* response made me realize what a fool I am. I plan to share it with Christiana and get her opinion. This will all be new to her since I've yet to mention that I began dating Miles.

Dear Fool in Love,

Love is never a mistake and giving it should never be a problem. If this wonderful guy doesn't reciprocate your feelings or is too closed off to admit his own in return, then you need to cut bait and run.

Don't stick around and try to love someone who isn't willing to return that love in spades. You're not the fool in this situation, he is.

Best of luck. I hope he realizes what he has before he loses it altogether.

All my best,

Ida

Honestly, I know all of this because it's straight from the pages of a Psychology 101 course, and the "if you love something, set it free" old adage. There's no going back once the words are out there. Miles needs to figure out what he wants from me in return.

I can't push him if he's not ready, and sadly, I don't think he is ready to get close to me or anyone else. He's still battling the demons of his sister's death and, for whatever reason, thinks he has something to do with it. Which is crazy because unless he gave her the heroin that she OD'd on, then he has nothing to blame himself for.

Christiana waves at me from the entrance of the bookstore, waiting for me with two coffees in hand as I approach her through Washington Square Park.

"Hey, Chica," she greets, leaning in to kiss me on the cheek before shoving an iced macchiato in my hand. "You look like shit. What's the matter with you?"

Leave it to Christiana to give me the no-filter blunt greeting. I give her a look of mock outrage and take a sip through the cup's straw.

"It's a good thing you come bearing gifts, otherwise I'd slap you," I tease, opening the door so she can walk into the building as I follow behind.

Her long raven hair bounces over her backside before she whips her head around to glance back at me.

"You want to sit down at a table for a bit before we get our books on?" She points with a finger toward the far right of the store where there are some empty tables.

After hanging my backpack over the back of the chair, I sit down to face her as she gets situated. I pull out my phone and place it on the table, opening up my email account so I can show her my *Ask Ida* messages.

"What's this?" Christiana nods toward the phone and then tips her head, brows furrowing in question.

Inhaling a deep breath, I let it out slowly and begin to tell her the story.

"Remember I told you how I ran into Miles the night of the fire alarm?"

She knows who Melodie is and is aware of my crush on

Miles, which I shared one drunken night early on in college, and how I ran into him the night of the fire alarm, but knows nothing of what's been going on since.

She nods, waggling her brows suggestively. "Of course, the hottie you crushed on hard. But wasn't he a dick to you?"

I may have also mentioned how rude he acted toward me. My goodness, how things have changed.

The thing about Christiana is that she holds back nothing when she's excited, angry, happy, or sad. All her emotions are worn on her sleeve, so it comes as no shock to me when she lets out a shriek of delight when I tell her we've hooked up.

"Holy shit, girl. You hoochie mama. Why the hell didn't you tell me this before? When did this happen? And when are you going to marry him and have his babies?"

Her voice is loud and carries through the area, so I slap my hand over her mouth and glare at her.

"Shh. Good lord, do you not have an inside voice?"

She snaps at my finger with her teeth playfully, and I pull my hand away, picking up the phone and handing it to her to read the *Ask Ida* inquiries.

"Here, read all about it."

She sifts through the messages, occasionally voicing commentary and *ooh's* and *ahh's*, and then slips in a few motherfucker curses in between. Finally, and with remorse written in her dark eyes, she hands it back to me as I chew on my lip, waiting for her wisdom.

We may have only been friends for a few years now, but she's like a sister to me, and I trust her for her blatant honesty and sage advice.

"I have to agree with *Ask Ida*. He's a sucker if he doesn't feel the same way about you and a coward if he slinks off because you said those three words. That's bullshit."

"But—" I try to interject, hoping to shed some light on Miles's good qualities and the potential reasons for his discomfort over this subject. Yes, I'm making excuses for him.

Her finger tick-tocks like a metronome in the air between us. "No buts. He's the one being a douchecanoe if he's dicking you around. Which means, sadly for you, no more dick unless the future becomes clear, and he admits his feelings."

I choke on the cold liquid I'd just sipped, furtively looking around to find a few people grimacing in disgust at Christiana's colorful language.

She snaps her head to the side and glares at a store employee and in a scoffing tone, asks the rhetorical question, "What? You've never had a guy be a dick to you?"

I return the phone to my purse, hunching my shoulders in defeat.

"I know I have to end things if he doesn't feel the same way. But in my gut, I feel like he does have the same level of connection. It's just tangled up in the other emotions that have a stranglehold on him since Mel's death."

Christiana draws me into her with an arm slung around my shoulder, side hugging me against her.

"You and I both know he's going to have to work that out on his own. You can't force it. He'll either come to the conclusion that he needs help in dealing with his unresolved grief, or he'll remain in the same pattern of loneliness that will only turn him into a bitter old man."

I avert my eyes, staring down at the table, my lips pressed in a firm line. I know she's right. She's smart and understands men since she has three brothers. But it doesn't make it any easier for me to let Miles go.

"Granted, he'll be a *hot* bitter old man, but bitter nonetheless, and it won't change things for you."

39

M*iles*

THE DINNER MEETING Graham and I had tonight with a potential client went well. Melissa Shauschenberg is the CEO of an online retail business that just went global, and she's looking to us to help her invest and increase her profitability through some strategic investments.

The only concern I have with Melissa as a client is that she is extremely flirtatious and handsy. The minute it came up in conversation that I was single, she angled and maneuvered her body so she'd inadvertently touch me or brush up suggestively. And she kept at it the entire time.

"If you have any questions about our proposal or the investment plans we can offer your business, please call us. Graham or I would be happy to review the terms with you in more detail," I say to her while we stand in front of Capicio's, the small Italian restaurant on the same street as our apartment building.

Melissa crowds me as if we're inside a packed train instead of the open sidewalk. She stands so close, in fact, that the firm curve of her breasts pushes against my arm every time she leans in to speak.

"Miles, you have no idea how much it means to me to be in such strong, capable financial hands with my investments. You and Graham seem so experienced and knowledgeable in these matters. I need men like you in my life." She says this in a throaty, raspy voice that is overtly sexual, sending fingers of dread trailing down my spine.

"Mmm-hmm," I absently agree, checking back over my shoulder to see what is taking Graham so fucking long to pay the bill.

Her hand suddenly leaves my chest, sliding over my dress shirt, groping my pecs and purring seductively. I think I'm a bit in shock, but just as she finds my belt, I grab hold of her wrist, stopping her progression.

This doesn't seem to deter her in the slightest, and she seems to take this as consent, moving closer and pressing herself against me as I look wildly around wondering if I'm being *Punk'd*. Is this what some women feel like in the workforce who are inappropriately fondled and degraded?

If so, #MeToo.

I'm about to speak up and push her away when I hear Sutton's soft, confused voice behind me.

"Miles?"

I turn, but the movement only brings Melissa along with me, who is still in my grip. I drop her wrist so fast she loses her balance and topples forward. I move to catch her and stand her upright, then let my hands fall to my sides. My hands clench into fists.

All the while, Sutton looks on with shiny, hazel eyes, blinking past the tears threatening to fall underneath her lashes.

"Sutton. What are you... ?"

There's a moment where I think she's going to turn and run, her fingers pressed to her mouth to cover her quivering lips. I know what she thinks she's seeing, but she's wrong. So, so very wrong.

I extend my arm to reach out, but she dodges it and steps back, all the while staring at me with eyes that tell me everything.

You're an asshole.

You hurt me.

I trusted you.

How could you do this to me?

I'm unable to respond to any of those questions or correct the misunderstanding because as people walk around and between us, a few times her face disappearing from my view, she finally steps forward and slaps me, figuratively, with her accusation.

"How could you, Miles? I thought I meant something. I thought you'd changed. If Melodie were still with us right now, she'd be so ashamed of you. You've humiliated me once again. I can't believe what a fool I've been. Thanks for letting me see the real Miles Thatcher."

The crowd dissipates just when Graham walks out the restaurant door to witness the conclusion of this scene. Sutton turns swiftly around and books it down the sidewalk as Graham steps up next to me, blocking my view, and stares at me.

"What did I miss?"

I have no words, but Melissa pipes in, "I think Miles just got dumped."

And sure enough, there's a first time for everything.

40

Sutton

TEARS TASTE LIKE SALT.

Salt can be bitter.

Bitter is how I feel.

Bittersweet is the feeling of not seeing Miles again.

I don't want to feel anymore.

My head remains buried under a pillow as I sprawl across the couch, where I've taken up residence for the past week since moving into my new apartment.

With the help of Ben, Christiana, and a couple of loads boxed up by Taylor, I moved into my new three-hundred-eighty-five square foot apartment in the West Village. With the money I'd saved from the Morgan's pet sitting job and the extra hours I'd taken on in Lucy's absence at the store, I was able to find a great second-floor walk-up in a cute red brick building, complete with a balcony and a window flower box. Plus, I'm just a few short blocks away from one of my favorite music venues, Webster Hall.

If only the beauty of that blooming floral arrangement and the possibility of seeing great upcoming acts at the theater was enough to make me feel better right now. To help me get over this heart-wrenching pain of what happened with Miles.

That night, I'd grown impatient and fed up with waiting for Miles to reach out to me, so I took the train to the Upper West Side and walked down the street to his apartment. But before I even made it to his building, I saw him coming out of the Italian restaurant he'd actually taken me to not even two weeks ago. And he was with another woman.

A beautifully dressed woman who was all over him.

I didn't want to overreact. That's not in my nature.

But something split open inside me, a chasm of frustration and disgrace, knowing that I'd been waiting by the proverbial phone to hear from him, all while he was apparently going out with other women.

God, I felt so broken and angry. I was inconsolable for days, while Christiana was at my side helping me pack and listening to me cry hot, embarrassing tears over a man I fell in love with.

And the part that hurts the worst?

I've received only two texts from him and one phone call, which I ignored.

Granted, the first one he did leave the ball in my court when he wrote: ***Sutton, please let me explain. Call me. We need to talk.***

The second one read: ***It's not what it looks like.***

Christiana scoffed when she read them as I cried my

eyes out with my head in her lap, sniffling like a baby who'd just lost her binkie. She commiserated with me, suggesting that I should let him hang because a "*let me explain*" approach was just a player's way of scheming their way out of being caught. It was a fabricated lie meant to gaslight the one who was cheated on.

So, I did what she said and let him stew in silence. The unfortunate problem for me, however, is that the plan backfired. I'm the one now sitting in silence, waiting to hear from him again. Waiting and hoping he'll have a logical explanation for what I ran into that night.

But now it's been over two weeks, and I've heard nothing more from Miles.

Nothing.

As if he's dropped off the face of the planet or has forgotten me as easily as he did in the past when I was just the invisible girl to him. So insignificant that he didn't even remember who I was when we ran into each other again less than two months ago.

At least during my broken-hearted grief, Lucy has kept me busy at the shop while she remains at home helping Antonio recover from his surgery. And my fall semester classes have started, leaving me trying to balance everything and keep my head above water.

It's overwhelming, but I have to keep busy. By keeping my mind off Miles, I avoid wallowing in my despair. Most of the time, anyway.

My phone pings with a message. I reach for where it's sitting on my coffee table. Picking it up and flipping it over, I notice it's a message from Ben.

Ben: Want to go to lunch today? My treat.

Me: Who put you up to this?

Ben: What? I have no idea what you're talking about. Just get your ass ready and meet me in an hour.

I scowl at the phone when he tells me where to meet him, knowing exactly who put the bug in Ben's ear. It was Christiana.

While Ben doesn't know anything about Miles and me, he is keenly aware that I'm down in the dumps, as evidenced by my sour mood when he helped me move. I'm pretty sure he was exchanging looks with the girls over my unusually quiet and sullen demeanor last weekend.

I shove the blanket from my legs and look down at my appearance. A brief sniff under my arms suggests I should definitely shower and don some new clothes before heading out. It takes all my energy to roll off the couch and push myself to get ready, but after I do, I feel some semblance of normalcy once again. I just wish the shower and change of clothes could as easily wipe away the pain still radiating like an open wound in my heart as it did the grime from my body.

Soon I'm heading out the door and making my way to the subway station. I'm meeting Ben at the greasy spoon he suggested for breakfast this morning. In most parts of the country, this time of day would be considered lunch, but on a Sunday, we New Yorkers tastefully call it brunch.

I see Ben from a distance, typing on his phone, his uncombed hair, wrinkled tie-dye shirt and army-beige shorts and sandals make him appear to look more like a fraternity boy after a late-night rather than a head marketing honcho for a Wall Street company.

"Hey, Sut," he says, pulling me in for a hug, his arms folding tightly around me and comforting me without realizing it. "Thanks for meeting me. I wanted to talk to you."

"Of course. About what?"

He looks away sheepishly as he hooks a thumb in the direction of the restaurant.

It's a glorious September day, the sun sprinkling its rays through the foliage of the park, the smell of street vendor food wafting around us, and just the barest hint of a cold breeze ushering through the late summer humidity.

We put our name on the wait list and stand outside where a small brunch crowd congregates, each waiting to hear their name called by the hostess.

"What'd you want to talk to me about?" I ask, pulling my hair over my shoulder into a ponytail.

"I wanted to ask your permission to, uh. . ." He hesitates as I lean in, tilting my head to the side, trying to figure out what he's getting at. "Well, I've gone out a few times now with Taylor."

"Taylor? My friend, the dancer, Taylor? That one?"

I'm stunned. While I was a complete zombie the day they helped me move, I vaguely remember them chatting and laughing together. Maybe even flirting. Memories of that day are hazey, but I can totally see them together.

Ben has always been a bit quiet and not a guy who would come on to a girl or be cocksure of himself with hubris. Not like Miles.

Ben nods, a smile now growing on his cute freckled face that makes him look like a comic strip kid. "Yeah. We kind of hit it off, and I really like her. But because you two are friends, I didn't want to make things uncomfortable for you."

I shake my head, affectionately grabbing for his hand and threading my fingers through his. "Ben, I think your thoughtfulness is sweetly adorable and speaks volumes of your character. But you do not have to worry about me or what I think. It's your life, and you should date, hook up with, hang out with, or fall in love with whoever makes you happy. This life we live is too short not to love and be loved by someone you care about."

That thought feels like I've just split wood with an ax, my chest being the wood.

Ben nudges me in the shoulder and throws his arm around me, squeezing in a brotherly gesture.

"Taylor wanted to tell you, but I asked her to let me do it. She didn't want you to be upset when you found out. Thanks for being okay with it."

I wave a hand in the air. "Please. I just want you both happy."

Our name is called, and we follow the waitress into the crowded diner, sliding into a table that's so cozy I'm bumping arms with the person next to me.

After ordering, we catch up on everything else when Ben brings up pet sitting at the Morgan's.

"Hey, Graham has been raving about you and the job you did while they were on vacation. I think you could get a ton of referrals if you want them. It might be a great side-gig for you. In fact, that reminds me, a few weeks ago or more, Miles came into my office to ask about you. I figured it was about the work you were doing, but then you guys had that altercation at the volunteer event, and honestly, I should've followed up. What the hell was it about?"

The mention of Miles's name causes my internal frequencies to jolt like a live wire, as if I'm being zapped at a million different puncture points. Hard, fast and stinging pain everywhere all at once.

I decide to come clean with Ben, having nothing more to lose.

"I guess I should tell you something too. You see, Miles and I knew each other from Mystic. His little sister was my childhood best friend. We ended up having a pretty big misunderstanding, but it got resolved, and then we actually started seeing each other."

Ben's head rears back as if dodging a ball that's flying at his face.

"No way! Wow, that's. . . you and Miles?" He gives me a skeptical look like I'm crazy. "I have to admit, you're definitely not a couple I'd imagine together."

I shrug a shoulder. "Well, you don't have to anymore because we're over. Things took a turn, and we fizzled out. Actually, burned is more like it. I realized there are things that have to change, and unless that happens, we're taking a break."

Really what I mean is that he has to decide to change.

But he hasn't. And he's walked away, not even willing to try.

Ben looks at me with pensive ale brown eyes. "Hmm. I'm sorry to hear that. I suppose you heard about his grandmother, then, right?"

I drop the fork that was in my hand and stare wide-eyed at Ben.

"No, what happened?"

He swallows and chews on his lip before answering. "Miles. . . he, uh, he's been out of the office rather unexpectedly. I guess his grandmother suffered a major stroke and is in intensive care. That's all I've heard. I'm sorry you didn't know."

The rancho huevos that I ordered and took a few bites of now sit like a rock in my stomach, threatening to return from where it came.

There are many unflattering things I've called Miles over the past weeks, but never would I say he was an unloving grandson. That woman is his world and the only remaining family he has left on this Earth.

If something happened to Iris and she passed on, I don't know how Miles would be able to deal with that. I fear that he would fracture under the burden of any more loss.

"Ben, I've got to go."

41

M*iles*

IF I HAD a choice between getting a root canal on an infected tooth without Novocain versus making the decision to end the life support that kept Granny alive, I would have chosen the dental procedure. It was one of the toughest choices I ever had to make, even with the letter stating no heroic measures already in Granny's paperwork on file. So when she had the stroke that left her in a coma, there was nothing to do except wait it out.

Graham came to visit one of the days before Granny died, and I spilled out my tale of woe. I shared with him my loss and feelings of failure over my sister's death. His sage advice, and subsequently the suggestion that I see a therapist, has started me down the right path.

"Bro, you've been through some pretty fucking tough times. Things I wouldn't wish on my worst enemy," Graham had said, slapping me on the back of the shoulder. "I'm telling you, you've got to learn to let that shit go, otherwise it will eat you alive until you're just a corpse inside. Don't hold onto that baggage. Move on and forgive yourself. Otherwise, you'll be a fucking bastard and pain in my ass forever."

His counsel, along with the discussions with my grief therapist have helped me to see there's light at the end of the tunnel. And now after my Granny's death, I need to say goodbye to all the women that I've loved in my life and let the past go with them. And maybe, if I'm lucky, I can make amends with Sutton. The only non-familial woman I've loved.

Pulling into the parking lot at Mystic Lawns Cemetery, I get out of the car and head toward our family's burial plots. Row upon row of headstones and placards greet me, some left unattended for years, and others cared for in a familiar and cherished manner.

Today is the anniversary of Melodie's death. A date, along with her birthday, that has haunted me for years, marking a day of self-loathing and guilt over the part I played in Mel's demise, overdose, and death.

My feet falter as I reach the row where my mother, Mel, and Granny's newly earthed gravesite reside. There's a fresh bouquet of flowers propped up against her headstone.

And there, sitting back on her heels, holding flowers and a photo in her hand, is Sutton.

Looking elegant, breathtakingly beautiful, and absolutely heartbroken.

"Button," I murmur, taking a few steps inside the green walkway toward her.

Her brilliant emerald eyes sparkle up at in the sunlight, her hand shielding her from the bright rays, as she turns her head to peer up at me in surprise.

She sucks in a gasp, and her mouth drops open as I bend down and plant a knee at her side.

"Miles, I'm so sorry about Granny. Had I known what happened, I would've been there for you. I swear. You shouldn't have gone through this alone."

Without hesitation, Sutton moves onto her knees and throws her arms around my neck, pressing her warm face into the crook. I take advantage of the moment and slip my arms around her waist, gathering her close as we exchange silent condolences to one another, honoring the woman who meant something to us both.

When I finally pull back, I notice a strand of hair that's escaped her ponytail, and I brush it off her face, tucking it behind her ear. My palm cups her cheek, retaining my physical contact with her, not wanting to let her go.

"What are you doing here?"

She sighs, sitting back again on her heels, flattening her palms on her thighs.

"Ben told me about your grandmother. And today is. . ."

"Mel's anniversary."

She nods, head hung low. "Yeah. I wanted to pay my respects and tell her that I still love her, and I'm sorry things turned out the way they did."

Inhaling deeply, I let it out in a big gush of air. "It's my fault she's dead, Sutton. All my fault."

Sutton gives me a defiant shake of her head. "You are not responsible, Miles. How could you be? We've talked about this before."

"Listen, Button. Will you go get coffee with me? I'd like to talk."

"You're seeing a grief counselor? Oh, Miles. I'm so glad to hear that."

I sit across the small outdoor cafe table from Sutton, sharing coffee and reminiscing when I tell her that due to her insistence, as well as Graham's, I've finally begun talking to a therapist and working through my loss.

I chuckle and deadpan, "You'd think I'd just said I won the lottery."

She peers through her lashes, blushing sweetly. "Talking about loss is difficult, but it gets easier, especially with a trained psychologist. And I'm happy that you found someone you can open up to and get things off your chest."

I extend a hand across the table and take hers, which she willingly gives.

"I was stubborn and didn't heed your advice right away. It wasn't until I was in the hospital room with Granny that it hit me. I physically had to let her go, and emotionally I had to sever the ties with Melodie, as well."

"Miles, will you share with me why you feel so responsible for Mel's death? I mean, you weren't even there when it happened."

Flipping her palm up, I trace the grooved lines of Sutton's hand, slowly navigating the lifeline around the curve of her thumb.

"Exactly. I wasn't there for her. I'd turned a blind eye to what was happening back home with Mel. I was in college, having a good old time, and ignored all the warning signs that were right there under my nose. Mel started skipping school. Her grades began to drop. She was getting detention and acting out. And then she quit the swim team, her favorite sport in the world. She had new friends and bad influences, leaving her good friends behind."

I cup both my hands around hers now, and she adds the

other to the mix. If someone looked, they'd think we were in prayer together. And maybe we are in some way. Purging ourselves of our sins and asking for forgiveness.

"I hadn't come home that summer like I'd done before because I stayed in the city with some friends. I regret that decision the most, looking back now. Perhaps if I'd been home, she wouldn't have started using. By the beginning of the school year, as you know, she'd all but dropped out. Mel called me the night she died."

I can't look Sutton in the eyes. It's too painful, and I don't want to see pity or contempt for my actions.

"I think she knew she was in trouble. She apparently went out that night to a party with an unfamiliar group of acquaintances. By then, I know she was drinking regularly, smoking weed, and taking pills. But that night, she tried heroin. Regardless of whether it was the first time or the hundredth time, it was the last. She got a dose of fentanyl-laced heroin—a lethal combination."

Button is openly crying now, dabbing her eyes with a napkin, her bottom lip trembling.

"Mel called me at some point that night. I'm not sure if it was before she got high or after. I didn't answer. I was busy. Too busy to make time for my only sister. I saw the missed called later that night around midnight and figured it was too late to call her back. Too late is right."

I take a breath and drop my head into my hand, keeping one attached to Sutton.

"I'll never have that chance to do it over again. It plays on repeat in my head all the fucking time, Button. I think you said it best. There are things we *shoulda, coulda, woulda* done to change the outcome of our life, but thinking about it in regret doesn't do shit."

"Miles, can I confess something to you?"

I lift my gaze to Sutton's face, whose smile is a pool of kindness. "Of course."

Her blush covers her soft features, a pink swath warming her cheeks.

"I never told Melodie that I had a crush on you because I thought she'd be mad at me. Or worse, tell you. But I believe she always knew. And I think that we're here together through fate and Mel. She's brought us together for a reason. Why else would we have reunited in this strange coincidental way after all this time?"

I nod in agreement. I don't think it's such a stretch to believe that, either.

Sutton continues, "I think Melodie is up there"—she points to the clear blue sky above us — "right this minute hatching some kind of plan, just like she always did when we were kids, to get us together. Is that weird to believe that?"

I smile fondly at Sutton because I feel the same way.

Lifting my coffee cup in a toast, prompting Sutton to do the same, I say, "Here's to fire alarms, fate, and family." We clink cups, and she grins from ear-to-ear.

"And here's to you, Button," I continue. "You are an unforgettable presence in my life. When I remembered the good memories of my childhood, of summertime and family, I saw you, Sutton. You were always present. And while those memories may have been buried for a while, I never really ever forgot you or what you brought into my life. You're part of me, then and now. And I love you."

EPILOGUE

T*hree-months later—Sutton*

"WELCOME! So glad you both could join us tonight."

Soraya stands at the entrance of their apartment door, arms open wide as she greets me and Miles, who's holding a bottle of wine in his hand, looking a bit uncomfortable by the very colorful greeting.

Until Graham steps out from behind the door and claps him on the back.

"Hey, man. Good to see your sorry ass. How ya been? It's been so long," Graham deadpans, looking to his watch facetiously with a laugh. "A whole three hours?"

They laugh and head into the living room while I follow Soraya into their large kitchen, which I put to good use while I stayed here in July. It's a Friday night in early December, and Graham and Soraya invited us over for an evening of food and games, which Miles scoffed at when he heard the part about playing games.

One of the things I've recently learned is that Miles has the attention span of a Labrador puppy when it comes to any sort of game. Unless it's watching the stock market rise and fall, he's not interested in fun and games.

Over the past three months, I've come to see how antsy Miles can be, never sitting for more than thirty minutes at a time and to him, playing cards or games, or heaven forbid, solving a puzzle, puts a strain of unease on him the likes I've never seen. I told him that he's a bit ADHD, and he scoffed at my applied psychology mumbo-jumbo.

"How are things going, Sutton?"

Soraya pulls out a large, chilled bowl full of colorful greens and a mixture of vegetables, retrieving a cucumber and a tomato from the crisper and setting them on the cutting board.

I pick up the knife and say, "Here, let me help you."

She gives a half-hearted shrug and a lopsided smile. "Help yourself. I'll put the rolls in the oven."

From over her shoulder, she asks, "Is school going well? And your side jobs?"

I nod enthusiastically. "Oh, yes. I love my classes this semester. Great professors and the topics are so much fun. My Human Behavior and the Social Environment class is so fascinating. I'm learning so much about human behavior and why people act the way they do in particular settings and situations."

I sound like a starry-eyed dope, but every day I learn something new that opens my eyes to the behavioral changes at different life stages. Miles has found my interest rather amusing and teases me about it all the time, now calling me his little Button book worm.

Soraya closes the oven door, sets the timer, and returns to the counter beside me. Next, she picks up a glass of wine, gesturing for me to do the same.

"Cheers," she says, clinking her glass against mine as we both take a sip.

Her smile is thoughtful, as her brows lift in amusement.

"I know exactly what you mean. Although I didn't go to school or get a fancy college degree, I see the aspects of the human condition every day in my line of work. Fascinating, indeed."

I nimbly slice the cucumber, as I ask absently, "Remind me what you do again? I think Miles mentioned that you're a newspaper columnist?"

"Yes, I write the *Ask Ida* advice column."

My knife stalls mid-slice, the piece of cucumber toppling over on its side with a wet thump, as my lips part in shock.

"Come again?"

Soraya snickers knowingly, shifting so her hip casually rests against the counter, arms crossed at her chest, glass in hand, cocking her head at me.

"The weekly advice column, *Ask Ida*. I receive some pretty interesting messages from readers, looking for advice on love, life, kids, marriage. The works. You'd be amazed at what I learn about people."

When I turn to look at her, I know my cheeks are burning bright red, and the expression on her face tells me she knows everything.

"Oh my God. Did you know it was me all along?"

I think back at the three letters I wrote and the responses she sent me. I never in a million years would have thought the person I was writing to and sharing my tales of woe with was the same person who hired me to pet sit her dog. Who is, at this moment, lies at Miles' feet in the living room, getting a belly rub.

"Well, yeah. They came from your email address, the same one you used to exchange messages while we were out of the country."

I smack my forehead, dropping my chin to my chest in mortified stupidity.

"You must've thought I was the biggest flake in the world."

Soraya laughs good-naturedly, extending a hand and placing it on the top of my shoulder.

"Honey, your letters were sweet, a little heartbreaking, but I never thought any less of you. And I can only assume, now knowing a little about yours and Miles's past, that you were writing about him?"

I nod quickly, glancing over my shoulder at the two men chatting and laughing in the living room, drinks in hand conversing over who-knows-what.

"Yeah, we have quite a shared history together. And there were a lot of roadblocks to get to where we are now. Mostly, the closer I seemed to get to him, the more I felt miles and miles away. He was closed off emotionally, and I knew I couldn't fix it for him. I ended up walking away, knowing it was the only way I could help him."

"You did the right thing," she agrees wisely. "It was a difficult thing to do, but look where things are now?"

We both turn our heads at the same time to see Graham and Miles smiling back at us.

"What are you two ladies chatting about in there?" Graham asks, his eyebrow cocked askew.

Soraya turns to me, and with a complicit smile and a gleam in her eye, says, "Fate."

The End

AFTERWORD

Want to keep up with all of the new releases in Vi Keeland and Penelope Ward's Cocky Hero Club world?
Make sure you sign up for the official Cocky Hero Club newsletter for all the latest on our upcoming books:
https://www.subscribepage.com/CockyHeroClub

Check out other books in the Cocky Hero Club series:
http://www.cockyheroclub.com

ACKNOWLEDGMENTS

First and foremost, thank you Vi and Penelope for this rewarding experience and opportunity to work with you and your team. Your support and feedback, along with the coaching you provided all your CHC authors, was beyond wonderful. This entire experience helped develop my skills as a writer and taught me how to work collaboratively to make a story happen.

And to the wonderful team at the CHC – including Dan, for his always helpful and immediate responses, as well as the support team that worked tirelessly behind the scenes. This couldn't have happened without you.

Much love and thanks to my editor, Missy, who helped me develop this story into something readable and entertaining. And Christine, my proofreader, who no matter what life hands her, manages it with a smile.

And finally, to all the Cocky Hero Club readers who love the Cocky Bastard series. I'm with you! I've loved this series from the very start because Vi and Penelope know how to weave such fun and fantastic stories for their readers. I'm blessed to have been able to write my own version within their shared world.

Thank you for reading my CHC story.

Be Sweet. Love Hard. Read Dirty.

xoxo, Sierra

ABOUT THE AUTHOR

Sierra writes new adult and sizzling hot contemporary romance. She's written and published over 25 novels, including the award-winning college sports series, ***Courting Love*** and the erotic ménage serial, ***Reckless – The Smoky Mountain Trio*** and most recently, her award-finalist new adult/college romance, ***Game Changer*** **(Change of Hearts Book 1)** is available NOW in ebook, print and audiobook.

Sierra lives with her husband and dog in the Seattle area. She is a sucker for cheap accessories, loves anything dark chocolate, and enjoys rocking out at live concerts.

Find all her books, her blog and Subscribe to her email list here: www.sierrahillbooks.com.

Made in the USA
Coppell, TX
20 July 2021

59204944R00162